AFTER HOURS

Maxey took a long drink of ice water. The noise of the restaurant suddenly rushed into her ears, as if two doors had opened. She caught Sam watching her, and gave him a seductive smile.

He leaned closer and murmured, "So what do you want to do after dessert?"

In case the question came up, Maxey had composed and rehearsed an answer earlier, not expecting to use it with honest regret. "I ought to go straight home," she said. "Tomorrow's an especially busy day at the office."

Sam drew back. "Whatever."

A vision of herself alone at the kitchen table typing came to Maxey's mind. She put her hand on Sam's wrist. "I said I 'ought' to go home. I'm open to suggestions."

Harper
Monogram

PRIVATE LIES

CAROL CAIL

HarperPaperbacks
A Division of HarperCollinsPublishers

This is a work of fiction. The characters, incidents, and dialogues are products of the author's imagination and are not to be construed as real. Any resemblance to actual events or persons, living or dead, is entirely coincidental.

HarperPaperbacks   *A Division of* HarperCollins*Publishers*
10 East 53rd Street, New York, N.Y. 10022

Cover photography by Herman Estevez

First printing: February 1993

Printed in the United States of America

HarperPaperbacks, HarperMonogram, and colophon are trademarks of HarperCollins*Publishers*

❖ 10 9 8 7 6 5 4 3 2 1

To my sister Julie:
For researching, cheerleading, and—way back ago—
playing what I wanted to play.

1

Maxey matched her fingers to the keys and typed: *Maxey Burnell, bored as a goldfish in a quart jar, on a Monday night in July, in Boulder, Colorado, sat down to write a novel, because that's what reporters are supposed to want to do.*

Sighing, she sank back in the kitchen chair and stared at the flotsam and jetsam of her life that covered the bulletin board in front of her. A clipping of Snoopy being a vulture on Charlie Brown's mailbox. A thank-you note from the third-grade class Maxey had visited on careers day. A snapshot of Maxey and her boss Jim and her ex-husband Reece in front of the newspaper office, taken by a Pearl Street strolling photographer, all three of them looking at least two sheets to the wind. A wallet-sized color portrait of her mother, who had managed to say cheese without smiling.

Undoubtedly Stephen King could transform this conglomeration into a novel. Damned if she could.

So okay, what she really wanted to do was phone someone, make a date to meet at Bennigan's or maybe a bar in Denver. Talk and dance and drink a couple drinks. Laugh. And stop wasting her precious youth on soliloquies.

Who to call? Duke Amory would jump into his Jeep and wheel straight over to squire her anywhere she said. No way. She would never take advantage of an old boyfriend that she had no intention of allowing to become new again.

Tim Rittenhouse? He had once invited her out, but she'd turned him down because she was waiting for Reece to make his move, and Tim seemed like the kind of guy who'd say, "I told you so." Which was definitely not what she wanted to hear tonight.

How about a female friend, then? Someone to talk to, and if the two of them happened across some male companionship during their night out, that would be okay. Bev Mayner.

Pushing away from the table, Maxey crossed to the telephone and consulted the flip-up list finder beside it. She dialed and turned around to lean against the counter, free arm hugging her waist. Glad to have thought of this, she tried to picture what was clean in her wardrobe.

"'Lo?"

"Hey, Bev, what'cha doing?"

"Who is it?"

"Sorry—it's Maxey. Well, no, I'm not sorry it's Maxey. You know what I mean."

"Gosh. I haven't talked to you forever."

"Yeah. I guess we've both been even busier than usual. So I was thinking how we ought to get together and catch up."

"Sure. When did you have in mind?"

Maxey stretched cord and arm to reach her cooling coffee cup. "I don't suppose you could make it tonight? Do a little barhopping?" She sipped, hoping.

"Oh, gee, we *have* been out of touch. I got married a month ago. Got a stepbaby now. You want to come for lunch one day and meet her?"

"Sure," Maxey said, her enthusiasm as false as her disappointment was real. "Lunch. I'll have to check my schedule at the office."

"Okay. Call me whenever."

"Right. A baby, huh? God!"

"Sheila's a joy," Bev began. "Let me tell you—"

"No. Don't tell me anything yet. Wait for lunch," Maxey said. "See you. Goodnight."

Now she had the added burden of guilt on top of her depression, knowing she would put off calling Bev until the kid was a teenager.

She slid the list finder down the alphabet, watching with increasing dismay as the blank or nearly blank pages were displayed. Giving up at

UV, she went to sit at the typewriter again, staring at the also empty page.

The open windows leaked intermittent traffic noise from Spruce Street while, in the alley behind, a lone shooter thumped a basketball at a garage-door hoop. Maxey's hard-of-hearing landlady on the ground floor was watching Channel Four news at full throttle.

The phone rang, and her startled twitch became a leap to answer it. Someone wanted to talk to her!

"Is this the Pizza Palace?" the nasal voice inquired.

"No," Maxey snapped. "You've got the wrong number."

"If it's the wrong number," the voice rose in complaint, "why did you answer?"

Leaving *Chapter One* in its entirety poised in the platen, Maxey went to bed to catch up on her beauty sleep. Another evening like this one and she would be absolutely gorgeous.

On Tuesday, hours west of Boulder, Rita Stamp opened her eyes. The sun pouring through the windshield batted them shut again. In the first fuddled moments of her return to consciousness, she thought that Jerald had stopped for a train. Its horn wailed so close, she forced her eyelids up and squirmed straighter to look, alarmed that the Buick might be stalled on the track.

There was the railroad track out her right window, on the far side of the Colorado River, and not a train in sight. Now she recalled being stopped behind a line of other vehicles waiting out a stretch of highway construction on the east edge of Glenwood Springs. Wiping sweat from under her chin with the back of her hand, Rita squinted at the spotty windshield.

The highway stretched empty.

The horn bleated again, and she jerked around. An endless chain of cars and trucks crowded at the Buick's rear bumper. The indistinct outline of the driver in the rusty station wagon immediately behind gestured with one finger. Rita's heart lurched her full awake. She stared aghast at the empty driver's seat beside her.

Where was Jerald? Hunching toward the windshield, she searched for his shape on the road ahead, but there was no one between the concrete wall on the left and the guardrail over the Colorado River on the right. She craned to see out each side window, growing as angry as the horns, that he had left her in this ridiculous position.

She remembered now; he'd shut off the motor when their lane was flagged to a stop. After a few minutes he got out of the car to join other motorists up and down the line looking into the wide, fast water. The last she'd seen him, he was resting his elbows on the guardrail, gazing across at the railroad track that hugged the cliff.

A car door slammed, and Rita's anger changed into panic again. Someone was going to say unpleasant things to her for holding up traffic. Her eyes slid to the ignition and pinched shut on the news that the fool had taken the key with him. A shadow covered the left front window.

"How about moving it, lady?" the man whined. He had a lumpy, hairy face, and a sunburned nose. "You can drive better from the driver's seat, did you know?"

"I can't go off without my husband." She copied his tone. "I don't know what happened to him. He got out and I went to sleep."

She waved helplessly at the windshield and, for a second, thought she could see Jerald coming, far down the road. But the figure jogging toward them wore a hard hat and a red vest, and was, as it drew closer, definitely female.

"Well, let's move this pile of junk over to the side, huh, and let everyone else get on with their lives?" the man said in the same snide way.

"I don't have the key. He took the key." She ducked her head to see up the stone beside the other, blocked-off lane. "Where could he be?"

She jumped under his shout of, "Give me a hand up here." He was calling to someone down the line. "We have to push it."

"You can't steer without a key." She didn't know much about cars, but she knew that much.

"We'll push it to where the road curves, and off onto the shoulder."

In her peripheral vision, many male shapes loomed. Arms stretched toward the sides and top of the car; feet scuffled on the gritty pavement. Throwing himself into Jerald's seat, the insufferable stranger knocked down the emergency brake. The girl in the hard hat had loped into shouting distance and she teetered to a stop to watch. The car creaked and began to roll.

"Wait," Rita wailed. "We have to find my husband!"

The man tipped outside to help push, holding the door open, ready to jump back in for the brake. Rita squeezed her eyes shut and heard involuntary grunts of effort, feet hitting the asphalt, the river racing beside. From some distant tree branch, a cardinal cascaded joy.

"Let her go," the man shouted.

When he leaped in to yank up the brake, Rita opened her eyes. The front tires rested on gravel side ditch, the hood aimed obliquely at gray metal railing. His exit made the chassis bob, and he was halfway back to his station wagon before Rita could make any appeals. Penned in by the guardrail, she had to risk impalement by the emergency brake as she crawled over it to the driver's seat to get out.

Across the road the hard-hat girl had a red-and-white sign on a short stick. She rotated the "slow" side toward the waiting line, and the bearded man's station wagon lunged forward, gnashing gears. As the parade continued she chewed gum and ignored the comments of masculine motorists appreciative of her tan skin and nonchalant stance while she eyed Rita across the tops of cars.

Rita walked to the rail and looked down. Beside the whitecapped river was a concrete bikeway and a portable toilet. Could Jerald be in there, sick maybe? She couldn't see any way to get to it from here. Her head began to ache in earnest from the light ricocheting into her eyes as she scanned and rescanned the landscape, expecting any moment to find him hurrying toward her.

Meanwhile the traffic sped by, blowing dust, carrying away any possible witness to his whereabouts. Rita wrung her hands, alternating between worry for and anger at her careless husband. She just didn't know what to do.

The hard-hat girl swung her free arm rhythmically, pumping cars through the single lane. When a slow gravel truck broke the flow long enough, she crossed the highway to continue directing traffic from in front of Rita's Buick.

"You need a tow truck?" she asked.

"I guess I need"—Rita revolved her head one more time, as if searching for a trail marker—"the police."

"What's the matter?"

"My husband has disappeared. We stopped when everyone else did, and a flagman came along the line to say it was going to be maybe a half hour's wait, and I went to sleep, and when I work up, Jerald was gone. Maybe he fell in the river."

Rita could feel the girl studying her, and that added to her misery. She knew how awful she must look in the wrinkled blue sundress, her blond hair limp and damp, her face too pink and legs too white.

The flag girl, who was slim and tanned under her layer of dust, unsnapped a breast pocket and hauled out a two-way radio. "Sector five calling sector one. Brinkman, you there?"

"Yeah, Amy, what you want?"

"We have a situation here about midway on the blockade. Lady's husband was driving when they got stopped and now he's gone and she's stranded."

"On foot?"

"Negative. She's got the car, but no key, apparently."

There was a meditative silence. A black-windowed Trailways bus swooped past, raising a miniature dust devil beside Amy's boots. In the middle distance a piece of heavy equipment screamed like a saw blade.

"Damn tourists," Brinkman finally said. "I'll send a tow truck."

"Uh, don't you think we ought to call the cops? What if he fell in the Colorado or a boulder dropped on him or something?"

Rita moaned.

It sounded a lot like Brinkman's grunt of disgust. "You know how much else I got on my mind today?"

"You know how much you'll have on your mind

tomorrow if we screw this up?" Amy stepped back a pace to spit her chewing gum into the ditch.

"All right, all right. Stay there till the smokey comes."

Amy put her radio away. Rita waited in the Buick, holding the door open with one foot, watching thirty minutes of backed-up traffic pour past. Virtually every vehicle in the relentless stream had at least one lookie-lou face twisted toward the possibility of tragedy.

The officer was baby-faced and excessively polite. Rita raked her eyes past his name badge— Douglas Timmey—in case she needed the information someday. She sat in the front seat of his air-conditioned patrol car and answered irrelevant questions like when was she born and where did she live.

She'd already described Jerald to him, and he'd relayed it somewhere on his car radio, though his jargon didn't sound like what she'd said at all, and she itched to take the microphone away from him and tell his colleagues herself.

The sun laid long flat shadows through the canyon now, and the hard-hat girl, Amy, had to shield her eyes from time to time as she directed traffic around the Buick and the strobe-sweeping cruiser in front of it. After Rita had answered all of Officer Timmey's questions, another patrol car nudged into the shoulder ahead, and she had to begin all over again with the new man, a John Moreno, who squatted by Timmey's open door, letting all the air-conditioning go to waste.

Except for an occasional speeding ticket, she'd had no experience with police. She'd pictured them briskly organizing a search, ordering up frogmen, perhaps. Dogs, maybe.

Instead they lolled about, interrogating her as if they thought she'd only imagined she was a passenger in her car going from Grand Junction home to Denver on I-70 through Glenwood Canyon with her husband at the wheel. Finally manners and timidity deserted her, and she said as much aloud.

"We're searching for Mr. Stamp right now, Mrs. Stamp," Officer Timmey said in his monotonously respectful voice. "The moment we find him, you'll know it by that radio there. We're going over the events with you several times in hopes you'll remember something new that will point out to us where he might be."

"We'd like you to think again about the time between when your husband shut off the motor and you fell asleep," Officer Moreno said. His voice was deeper but just as solicitous. His black hair looked like he'd been standing in a breeze with his foot on someone's bumper. "You say he sat a moment with you, just waiting?"

She nodded. The tissue she held to her mouth had deteriorated to a holey, damp lump. She longed for coffee.

"Was the radio on?"

Shaking her head, she pictured a tall, sweating glass of iced tea.

"Did Mr. Stamp say anything at this point?"

"No." And a cheese Danish.

"Did you say anything at that point?"

"No. I was half-asleep already."

Officer Moreno scribbled in his little memo pad as if she'd said something profound. "And then the state employee came by to tell everyone there'd be about a half-hour wait. And how long after that was it before your husband exited the car?"

"Two, three minutes. We'd had time to shut off the motor and roll down the windows. Others got out first. People were strolling up and down the road, sight-seeing, like it was a boardwalk. Jerald said, 'Want to look at the rapids?' and I just waved to show I was too tired, and he got out. The door latched. He walked in front of the car to the railing and stood there watching over the side. That's when I dozed off."

"Did anyone speak to him or did he speak to anyone?"

She licked her lips and rubbed her forehead. "Maybe. I heard male voices from time to time. They were too low for me to make out the words."

Officer Moreno adjusted his aviator sunglasses. "Can you recall anything that was said?"

She wanted to shake him and tell him to pay attention. With exaggerated patience she repeated her last sentence.

A highway-department pickup jiggled over the distant horizon, coming at them in the far, blocked-off lane, throwing dust like a cavalry charge. Rita fixated on its windshield, expecting Jerald's face to materialize there.

"Here he is, ma'am," the driver would say. "Got hit on the head by falling rock and temporarily lost his memory. But he knew his wife's name, all right. It's all he's been saying—'Rita, Rita—' "

Then her middle-aged husband of twenty years would give that annoying shake of his key ring that signaled he was about to drive off in the car somewhere, and she'd trade this cigarette-tainted vehicle for her own, which smelled of Jerald's after-shave, and they'd ease into the eastbound string of cars and discuss it all to death on the way into Denver.

The truck was close enough now for her to see there was only the driver, who waved at Amy as he barreled on past.

Rita swatted blindly at the near door, found the handle, and wrestled it open.

"Mrs. Stamp?" the deputies said in harmony.

"I'll find him myself," she said, indulging in a mighty slam of the door. Jerald had better be hurt or he was never going to hear the last of this.

2

Grady Feders told Josie Villa he was going to fix the toilet in number twelve, and then he locked himself in the room and installed the infinity transmitter in the telephone. It would have cost him as much as a thousand bucks to buy under some shady counter, but he'd made it himself for less than a hundred.

Applying two more twists to the screwdriver, checking that the alligator clips were snug, snapping the casing into place, and screwing it to the base—it all felt exhilaratingly satisfying, like the one time he'd hit a home run in Little League.

He sat on the foot of the king-size bed and, twiddling the screwdriver, surveyed his domain.

White walls, white ceiling, maple woodwork, navy drapes, navy bedspread, color-TV set fastened to a laminated credenza, assorted lamps, two scarred bedside shelves, aluminum luggage rack, and around the corner, a five-foot-square bathroom. And one bugged phone.

Collapsing backward, he stared at the ceiling tiles, speckled so the dirt didn't show. What if nobody stopped this evening? First one who did, no matter what he and/or she looked like, they'd get room twelve. It was the fanciest device he'd had so far, and he could hardly wait to try it out.

The outside door reverberated slightly, which Grady recognized as one of Josie's timid knocks. He bounced off the mattress, stuffed his tools into back pockets, and swagger-walked to unlock it.

Josie had retreated five steps toward the office, hands clasped as if she was about to sing an aria. She'd been in the United States six months, and all the English she'd learned would fit into a taco shell with space left over for extra beans. Grady didn't know much Spanish, but that wasn't his problem.

"Mama Weenie," Josie announced, putting one fist to her ear, the little finger extended toward her mouth.

Why learn English when she was so good at charades? He nodded and snapped the door shut. She retreated off the sidewalk to let him have an unobstructed three-foot width to himself. Anyone watching would think he beat her. It wasn't personal, though; Josie was afraid of everybody.

The one human being Grady feared was "Mama Weenie." He let the office door bang behind him as he reached across the counter to lift the phone.

"Hi, Winnie."

"Grady, did you do what I told you?"

"What's that, Mom?" He wiped dust out of the push-button crevices with a bare forefinger.

"Did you call city zoning?"

"Yes," he lied. "The man I needed was out."

"You don't need a man, for chrissake. Just ask them for a map." Her deep voice scoured his ear. "They surely got a map that shows the zoning boundaries. You don't need a man till we see if there's a problem." She barked her smoker's cough.

His mother sounded like a man. She looked like one, too, with her chopped-short white hair, flat, angular figure, and shrewd, squinty eyes. Since retiring and handing over the reins to Grady two years ago, Winnie lived in a cabin at Red Feather Lakes and spent her time fishing, playing gin, and thinking up obstacles to Grady's happiness.

Recently she'd had this crummy idea of turning the motel into offices. If Grady was lucky, he could sabotage and stall her for a year or so. Or she might get mad and come to Fort Collins and do the job herself inside of a week.

"Okay," he said. "I'll go get some literature. How's the weather up there?"

"Don't put it off, Grady. Call me when you have the information."

She hung up without a good-bye, as usual. Grady deliberately relaxed his stranglehold on the receiver and gently returned it to the cradle.

The motel didn't bring in much money, but it was enough to buy groceries. And support his electronics hobby, which his mother didn't realize the proportions of.

When he asked her why she wanted to take away his livelihood, she'd said, "You can get a job in hotel management easy, with your experience."

"Would you want to go work for somebody else after running your own place?" was his useless appeal over the telephone, as usual. She hardly ever came to town, thank goodness.

"Your father and I started Come On Inn from scratch, five years before you were born," she said, reciting the same old chapter and verse. "Many's the time we wished it was someone else's headache, that we could just put in our nine to five and go home and forget it. So here I'm doing you a favor! Besides, you don't own the place—you work for me. What's the difference if you work for someone else?"

He couldn't wire the rooms, *that* was the difference.

Grady's one pleasure in life was fooling with electronics. It had begun in high school, when he should have been discovering girls, and it had been his mistress ever since. Uninterested in sports, not a member of a gang in any sense of the word, he'd been the shy, quiet kind who was happy to get a *C* in anything. Bearing an unfortunate resemblance to Anthony Perkins, he'd grinned and borne the references to Bates Motel, and even the gibes about the Cum Inn. Mostly he drifted along till the day he met his first voltmeter in Electronics 101 and discovered life's intentions for him.

He still couldn't spell, juggle numbers, write a legible sentence, or string a dozen of them into a speech. What he could do was read schematics, assemble boards, solder joints, splice wires, test circuits. He could whip through a kit or invent something on his own.

When he'd mastered radios, generators, robots, and tesla coils, he moved on to more exotic, necessarily clandestine, projects: a pulse TV device that, secreted in the hand, would completely disrupt picture and sound, which Grady gave to a friend because he was too chicken to use it against his parents. A microblitzer stun gun ("stuns with 75,000 volts of power—for unruly animals only") that crackled and sparked so viciously when he tried it on a tree trunk, he buried it in the bottom of a bureau drawer. A little box that simulated tone frequencies for the coins used in pay phones, so that calls could be placed to anywhere for free, but which Grady also hid away after realizing he had nowhere to call.

He pleased his parents with a "guest sensor" that glowed red on top of the living-room TV when anyone came into the adjoining office, and they even reimbursed him for a similar device that signaled someone had driven under the portico.

And then, when he was a junior in high school, he mail-ordered ($19.95, allow six weeks for delivery) a kit that would automatically record all phone calls, incoming and outgoing, no batteries required. Pretending to be an FBI agent, he installed it between the office phone and a cheap cassette player in his room. It told him what he was going to get for his birthday, which unmarried neighbor lady was pregnant and by whom, and how widespread his father's cancer had become before even his father knew.

Thinking of all those virgin phones in Come On Inn's twenty rooms, realizing the infinite possibilities for entertainment that the constant rotation of guests would provide, Grady began allotting every available penny to acquiring a smorgasbord of surveillance gadgetry.

As soon as his mother was widowed and he was graduated, she abdicated management but not ownership of the motel to Grady. He had a hard time maintaining a sober face during the three weeks it took for her to move out. Another three weeks later, his old bedroom had been converted into a full-fledged spy headquarters where he could monitor each new bit of equipment as it was created and installed.

He had no two bugs alike. Some used hard wiring, some batteries, some line-carrier transmission. They were located in phones or wall receptacles, or built into a lamp or picture frame. Most of them picked up not only phone conversations but any other sound within the room's four walls. He received on tape recorders, an air-band radio, an ordinary FM radio, a spike mike. Wearing headphones, cuddling a beer, watching the play of light on the ceiling from a soundless TV, he listened to strange voices, unfamiliar names, odd accents, coughs and burps and groans.

It wasn't the ends that fascinated him, it was the means. He compared each type of installation for cost, clarity, range, ease of installation, life of transmission—not just in his head, but meticulously in extra-fine ballpoint pen in a five-by-eight spiral memo pad. He scarcely listened to the dialogues of his unwitting customers, and their sexual commotion was more often disgusting than titillating. He wasn't a voyeur or a snoop; he was simply a surveillance virtuoso.

But sooner or later Winnie would win. His secret base of operations would have to be dismantled to make room for strangers' offices, and he would have to seek employment in the real world.

He'd be afraid to apply for a job with the FBI. Instead of marveling at his self-taught expertise, they'd probably arrest him for illegal activities.

As it turned out, Grady knew the first customer to stop that evening. An office-products salesman for a wholesaler in Salt Lake, Errol Sarfield stayed at the Come On Inn every three months on his way to Nebraska.

"'Lo, Grade-A," he sang out, strutting into the office like it was a Hilton and he was in *Who's Who*.

Grady looked up from the *Post* between his elbows on the counter. He smiled with some reservation, never able to warm completely to anyone who would decorate his bumper with a sticker reading *Shit Happens*.

Sarfield tossed his credit card on the counter and sawed at his necktie. A short man with a square, meaty face and reddish hair that always needed combing, his mood usually on the edge of irritability, he reminded Grady of a Pekingese.

"Give me the usual."

The "usual" was room twelve, but Grady hesitated, unwilling to inaugurate the new equipment with someone as boring as this lone salesman was bound to be. He printed on the credit-card slip with laborious gouges of the ballpoint.

"Hot, hot, hot." Sarfield put one hand on a hip and stared out at his dusty '84 Olds. "I had a stop to make in Grand Junction this morning, so I came over on Seventy. Had a half-hour wait at Glenwood Springs. Now that was hot. How much longer before they get that road done?"

"Years. I forget."

Grady read over the charge slip before turning it and the pen toward Sarfield, who signed with five sweeping loops and a period. Two turquoise-and-silver rings didn't improve the looks of his freckled, pudgy fingers.

The key with its indented "12" hung on its appointed hook. If Grady didn't give it to Sarfield, there would probably be no one else to give it to that night. It was the kind of small disappointment that usually littered his life.

"Number twelve, your usual," he said, offering the key.

Sarfield put it in his mouth while he returned credit card to wallet. The tag dangled like a dead mouse.

Twenty minutes later Grady was mentally kicking himself as he filled out the registration for an out-of-sorts diminutive blonde and her determinedly cheerful, British-accented husband. Betting their conversation would sizzle his ears, he put them in with the next best bug, the hot mike in room fifteen. Between their exiting shoulders, Grady noticed Sarfield's Olds spitting gravel as it turned left into town.

In the next couple of hours he filled eight other rooms of the Come On's twenty. A good night. And any of them would be more of a test of the new equipment than the TV-and-snore that Salesman Sarfield undoubtedly had planned. Oh, well, tomorrow would be another night.

Check-ins were few or nonexistent after nine-thirty. Preparing to get comfortable, Grady rustled a package of potato chips out of the cupboard and swept a pair of beer bottles, one-handed, from the refrigerator. Setting the refreshments beside his earphones on the bedroom desk, he considered, picked up the beers again, and returned to the kitchenette to replace them with a pitcher of lemonade. In the office he dumped two days' junk mail out of the ice bucket, straight-armed the counter's swinging gate, and exited onto the concrete loading zone.

The ice machine was halfway up the line of rooms, interrupting the perfect monotony of door, window, door, window, door. . . . The couple in room fifteen were fulfilling Grady's expectations. He didn't need a microphone to hear her grievances regarding hubby's not stopping earlier and then stopping *here.* Like a musical refrain, the object of her wrath kept repeating, "Will you bloody well shut up?"

Grady reached his destination and slid the sweaty metal door open. As ice thunked into the plastic bucket the machine cycled on, drowning out other sounds. A headlight swept across him, and Grady half turned to identify Sarfield coming home. The salesman nudged his Olds into number twelve's allotted space and shut off the engine, but didn't get out.

Curious, Grady scooped another measure of ice that he didn't need and watched Sarfield sit in his car. There was movement on the passenger side, and Grady grinned to himself. Maybe the new transmitter would get a workout after all.

Once before, Sarfield had contracted for a single room and used it as a double, undoubtedly thinking he was putting something over on the management. Grady strolled up the gritty sidewalk, enjoying this rare occasion of being totally in the right, and bent to look in Sarfield's window. The woman, in shadow, had short hair and big ears.

"Nice night," Grady said. "Have a good supper?"

Sarfield had to clear his throat. "Yeah, and the best part about it was I ran into an old friend and fellow drummer. We brought back a six-pack for a confab."

"Uh-huh." The ice bucket Grady was clutching to his chest oozed cold air under his chin.

"Say," Sarfield said as if he'd just thought of it. "Have you got a room for the night, Terry? Grady, here, probably has some still available."

Terry mumbled.

"Okay," Sarfield continued in the falsely cheerful tone. "I'll run you over there when we're through here." He unlatched the door and Grady stepped back.

Instead of getting out, Sarfield turned to his companion and asked for a cigarette.

Grinning at the salesman's obvious reluctance to be seen with Terry, Grady walked on to the office door and swished it open. When he glanced back, Terry was bending to get out of the car, unaided by Sarfield. She was either very ugly or a man.

Grady bruised a hip on the kitchen table, rushing to don his earphones.

At about this time Maxey was dialing her telephone.

"Hi, Tim? This is Maxey Burnell."

The ensuing pause was a fraction too long. Then: "How ya doin', Maxey?"

"Not too shabby. I guess you heard that Reece and I split."

"I could've told you so. Not to trust that—"

"Yeah. Listen, I was thinking of doing a write-up on dirt skiing, and I thought of you."

"Dirt skiing? What's that?"

"Or whatever it's called. You know, skiing down a bare slope in the summer. Didn't you try that one time?"

"Mm. No, wasn't me."

"Oh." She stared out the kitchen window. The alley below was all shades of gray.

Tim breathed into the phone. Rock music throbbed in the background.

"Sounds like you're having a party," Maxey prompted.

"Nope." More breathing.

"I'll let you go now," she said, blacking out his name in her list finder.

3

Rita Stamp dropped in a hard blue plastic chair, too tired to care anymore where the hell Jerald had gone.

Cold coffee in a soft foam cup sat on the metal table, perilously close to her elbow. Every five minutes or so a policeperson would stick head in doorway of the bare little cubicle and ask some illogical question. (Does Jerald smoke? Did he ever do any camping? Would you like another cup of coffee?)

Feet tramped up and down the hallway. Disembodied voices joked, cursed, droned. Doors banged. Typewriters and telephones beeped. She should have been home by now, supper dishes loaded in the washer, settling down with the *Post* and a "Golden Girls" rerun.

A kid in a three-piece suit bustled in, balancing a coffee mug on a manila folder. Sawing out the other chair, he sat beside her, crossed his knees, repositioned her cup out of harm's way, and avoided looking at Rita by studying the folder's contents. He had fuzzy blond hair, invisible eyebrows, and girlish hands. Rita didn't look at his name badge, having stopped trying to memorize names hours ago.

"Mrs. Stamp, your daughter is here to take you home. I just want to cover a couple key points here before you go."

She nodded, propped-up fist pushing her cheek out of shape. That was all she needed. Janice squirming and twittering and speculating the whole trip to Denver.

"Here's a key that fits your car, courtesy of the local Buick dealer. I believe it's your son-in-law who's come along with her to ferry it home for you."

Now that was all. All she needed. Bossy Bertie Goodman to tell her what she should have done.

"We're going to get a diver in the river tomorrow, just to eliminate that possibility, you understand. Since the dam and power station are just a mile or so downriver, the area of search is narrowly confined." He closed the folder and finally looked her in the eyes. "I know you may have answered these same questions several times. But not to me. Please bear—"

"Okay," she said, chugging along on resignation.

"Why was it you were in Glenwood Springs?"

She sighed. "Jerald's a soap salesman. Grand Junction's part of his territory. For once he'd taken me along on an overnight sales trip. We were coming home. Glenwood Springs is in the way." She meant "on the way," but somehow "in" seemed more fitting.

The policeman pursed his mouth. "What kind of soap?"

Well, at least this irrelevant question was one that nobody else had asked her. "Rest room," she snapped.

"Can you think of any reason your husband would have wanted to disappear?"

"No."

"Not in trouble with the law?"

"No."

"Not terminally ill?"

"No."

"Marital difficulties?"

"No."

"Money problems?"

"No." She was on total automatic now. He could ask her if she wanted a date with Tom Selleck or a million dollars tax free, and she'd have said, "No."

"How about enemies? Can you name anyone at all who had some quarrel with Jerald?"

He stiffened as she gasped and wailed, "Nooo!"

She had cried—who wouldn't—at about six

o'clock, when the hope of quick solution abruptly gave way under her. But this new grief that struck her was the worst yet. Wanting her long-dead mother, Rita put face in arms on table and could not be comforted.

It looked as if she and Jerald would never ever fly to Hawaii when he retired.

Maxey was brushing Watermelon Pink on the next-to-the-last nail when the phone rang. And rang. Seeing that she'd failed to set up Ernestine the Answering Machine, she lifted the receiver carefully, fingers splayed at all angles.

"Evening, doll," the caller purred. "How's my favorite girl reporter?"

"Hi, Bradley."

"All alone?"

"At the moment." She imagined his heavy-handed after-shave seeping through the phone lines with his voice.

"Got a message for you. Straight from *Romeo and Juliet*. You ready? 'The time and my intents are savage-wild, more fierce and more inexorable far than empty tigers or the roaring sea.' Provocative stuff, huh?"

Reece had once remarked that Brad's hairdo looked a quart low.

"So how about it, Maxey? Want to get together for whatever happens? Shall we say tomorrow night?"

"Let me look at my calendar." Maxey put down the receiver, picked up the nail polish, painted the tenth nail, blew on it, picked up the phone. "I'm sorry, I've got something scheduled every night for the next month."

"I'm impressed. Busy lady, huh?"

"Yeah. But I'm glad you called."

She was, too. Hanging up, she hugged herself, laughing, overjoyed to discover she wasn't that desperate yet.

The new infinity transmitter in number twelve worked like a dream.

When Grady skidded to a stop at the bedroom desk, carelessly depositing the wet ice bucket in the middle of the bedspread and lifting the coded activator with some reverence to dial the bugged phone in twelve, he'd actually shivered with anticipation. Quickly, before the phone could ring, he pressed the activator against the mouthpiece of his own handset, signaling the line that the called phone had been answered, transforming the still-cradled receiver into a bug that would pick up conversation within a twenty-five-foot radius and pour it into Grady's waiting ear.

The first sounds were intermittent—sighs, chuckles, clicks, zips.

"Terry," Sarfield said.

Grady had just turned up the volume, and he

jerked with the explosive word, reaching frantically to twist the dial in the opposite direction.

"Terry, Terry, Terry."

The quality of the reception made Grady laugh out loud. Every consonant, vowel, pause, and implication was clear as a bell.

"Let's compare," a voice like Winnie's growled. "I'm longest, so I get dealer's choice."

"Whatdayamean? I never heard of—"

"Just shut your trap and listen. I want it me across the bed with my legs on the floor and you down on your knees between."

"Let's have some beer first, what do you say? There's no need to rush—"

"And ice. That guy had some ice."

"You want ice in your beer?" Sarfield sounded shocked.

"Not for the beer. For me. Here and here. And in here. Oh, yeah, lots of it in here. Hurry up before I come without you."

Grady could hear each individual floorboard creak, the tumblers in the door lock, the scrape of door on sill, even the hum of traffic on the road outside as Sarfield went out.

The next half hour Grady hunched over the desk, forgetting refreshments and the ice bucket puddling the bed, admiring sound fidelity as Sarfield and Terry debased themselves with one another. That this was a homosexual escapade, a rarity in Grady's experience and one he strongly disapproved of, scarcely intruded on his listening pleasure.

The IT and its hookup were the best he'd ever done. He longed to brag to someone all about it.

When the loverboys had used each other up, Terry announced he needed a ride "back," and Sarfield churlishly told him to catch a bus. Terry left—*thump, thump, ka-rack, slam*—and Sarfield went into the bathroom and latched the door — *pad, pad, pad, ca-snick*.

Grady stretched extravagantly backward in his chair. Before calling it a night, he ran all the rooms one time, plugging into the various radios and receivers, expecting nothing.

Snoring. TV. A furiously thumping mattress in Blondie and Brit's room. Silence, silence, TV, silence.

"So what's your name, honey?"

The sly, soft voice came from eighteen. Grady fiddled the volume up and held his breath.

"Still not talking, huh? How come you won't trust me? Have I made one wrong move your direction? Huh? No. Forty-five minutes I sit here letting you squirm and cry and try to get your courage up. Have I touched you? No. But I'm just human. Hu*man,* get it? You going to let me sit a little closer? Good. Now I'm going to take your hand, and, see, that doesn't hurt. Where'd you put the money? You think I gave you that so's I could sit and watch you cry?"

The wheedling monologue was punctuated by feminine peeps of answer that would have been a cinch for the new IT to pick up, but the battery in this old wireless transmitter was low, and Grady grimaced, trying to hear.

"Here we go now. Last button. Ah-ah, easy. Damn it, hold still."

Grady pursed his mouth, picturing who it was he'd given the key to this single room. A white man, sport shirt, quiet, balding, Ford Escort.

The female voice sirened one, cutoff wail.

"I'm losing patience, you understand me? You got my money and now I get you."

"Furs time, furs time," she babbled, and Grady's neck hairs stood at attention. He pushed up from his chair.

"Bullshit," the man observed, breathing as if he was jogging.

The bed squeaked and so did Josie Villa. *"Tengo dolor de cabeza! Tengo"*—audible swallow— "headache!"

"Don't worry, I don't need your head." A bass chuckle. "Well, maybe a little head." More scuffling. "Okay, leave that on if you want."

Grady's eyes glazed at the blank wall above the desk. Should he break his rule of uninvolvement and walk down to number eighteen and save Josie from prostituting herself? Dumb Mex. She probably thought the guy was trying to buy cigarettes.

Hesitating, hating the possibility of an embarrassing scene, wondering how to answer if the john wanted to know how he knew Josie was in there,

Grady seesawed indecisively from one foot to the other.

"*Owwww!*" Josie screeched, and Grady ripped off the earphones in self-defense.

Okay, so he happened to be passing by and heard that scream. Okay, so he happened to have a crowbar—he rooted it out of his toolbox—in his hand.

Striding through the apartment and the office and out into the night, Grady felt two things he'd never felt before. Strong and brave. He could construct a hell of a bug, by God, he thought, tapping the crowbar menacingly on one palm. Strong and brave and *smart*.

He prowled purposefully along the building front, in and out of shadows, glancing sidelong at the mostly darkened windows. In front of sixteen his legs took smaller steps, carrying him more slowly to the confrontation. A crack in the drapes of eighteen revealed light but nothing more. Grady bent an ear to the soundless door before tapping on it with four knuckles.

"What?" came the muffled, irritated answer.

"Open up. Manager." Grady throttled the crowbar with both hands.

Silence lasted until the chain rattled and the door jumped open. Up close, the man looked bigger than Grady had remembered, and the sport shirt was gone, but he was still balding, with a chest to match.

"What?" he said again.

"I have reason to believe," Grady began, standing extra straight and feeling like the Equalizer, "you have a young woman in there against her will."

"It was her idea and none of your business, bub."

Grady poked the crowbar between frame and closing door. "Let me talk to her."

The man snorted and ran a hand through his nonexistent hair. "Good luck there, sport."

"Josie?" Grady raised his voice toward the guy's left shoulder.

"Grady—Grady—Grady—Grady," she said. She'd never called him anything but "Meester" in the past.

A flicker of doubt wrinkled the man's forehead, and Grady crowbar-pried him off to the side. Josie stood beside the rumpled bed, wearing black panties and clutching everything else, including shoes, to her chest. Later Grady would have time to realize she had a much nicer shape than her uniform had led him to believe. At the moment he was too busy watching the john for sudden moves.

"Out," Grady told her, making shoveling motions toward the night behind him.

Nodding, sniffing, stumbling, shying, Josie came over and out.

"You know how old this kid is? Fifteen. Sixteen, tops," Grady fabricated.

Josie batted her wet eyes, giving a good impression of bewildered youth.

"Oh, for—" The man prepared to slam the door.

"I want *you* out of here, too," Grady said, flush with easy victory. "And don't come back." He turned to squint meaningfully at the license plate of the Escort nosed in at the sidewalk. "Or I call the cops."

When the man scraped a hand down his jaw, Grady was amazed and delighted to see it was shaking. The trembling journey continued on down to scratch at bare belly, farther still to jab into a pants pocket and dredge out a wallet.

"Here," the man said, lifting three twenties out into the space under Grady's nose. "All the cash I have on me. No trouble."

Hypnotized, Grady reached for the bills.

The money retreated a few inches while the man repeated, "No trouble."

"No trouble."

The twenties slipped into his fingers. The door closed in his face. The crowbar, forgotten, clanked hard across his toes. Grady looked over at Josie, who was just checking her own fistful of money.

She tweaked her mouth in the closest thing to a smile she'd ever shown him and painstakingly said, "Good badger."

Well, of course it wasn't a badger game. He and Josie hadn't plotted this out in advance. It was all just a dumb misunderstanding. Still, it was the quickest sixty bucks Grady had ever made. Back in his bedroom, as he began the routine of switching off receivers, he paused to ponder the earphones in his hand.

Absently he sat on the edge of the bed, thinking of how, about a year ago, he'd recognized a state senator waiting in a black Caddy while his "wife" signed them in under aliases. Since Grady wasn't interested in politics, he'd only heard their indiscretions with half an ear as he experimented with reception on an air-band radio. Now he just bet that guy was carrying more than sixty bucks in his wallet.

Another time a fellow who identified himself as a Wyoming detective transporting a prisoner to Albuquerque had left the next morning alone, due east, while his charge thumbed a ride in the southbound lane, no doubt continuing the trip to prison on his own. As Grady thought about it now very large sums of money had been the topic late into the night.

Money was something else that had never much interested him except when he needed to finance some new electronic toy. But since Winnie had this mouse up her pants leg to convert the motel into offices, money had acquired a whole new priority. Grady was soon going to be out on his listening ear. Unhoused and unemployed.

Unless. Unless he got his own motel somewhere somehow.

He sat thinking for so long that one foot went numb and had to be stamped awake. When he went into the bathroom, the fluorescent light buzzed and stuttered, making his reflection in the medicine-cabinet mirror flicker like an old movie.

He'd need a better recorder. Maybe even a peephole camera. It wouldn't be blackmail. It would be helping wrongdoers pay for their mistakes. Just until he had enough for a down payment on a motel.

And maybe a car.

4

Three days later Maxey hunched over a telephone in the *Blatant Regard* office, absent-mindedly gazing at her ex-husband's crotch. It was a very nice crotch, with just the right amount of roundness stretching the blue jeans, and her right brain was bragging, "I've seen him naked."

To which her left brain was remonstrating, "Yes, and so have a dozen other females in the greater Denver area."

Out loud Maxey had to ask her caller to repeat the question.

"I want to know if it's safe," the old lady shouted, as if Maxey were hard of hearing instead of only short on attention span. "The electric company wouldn't tell me, because of course they want to sell all the electricity they can."

"You're going away on vacation. And you're afraid to leave the power on. Because—" Maxey faltered, afraid to go on, in case it wasn't what the woman had said.

But it was. She said it again. "I don't want it to leak out into the room."

"Uh, why doesn't it leak out while you're at home?"

"Well, because we're using it and it doesn't have a chance to build up," the woman snapped, obviously disappointed that the expert she'd phoned for advice was turning out to be such a dimwit.

Reece pulled open a file drawer between him and Maxey, spoiling her view. "I can assure you, Mrs."—she consulted her scribblings on the junior legal pad—"Jaspin. There's not one drop of electricity going to seep out while you're gone."

Reece snorted. Across the cluttered room, Jim Donovan glanced up and shook his head without missing a beat on the computer keyboard.

"I guess I *could* cover the outlets with masking tape," Mrs. Jaspin said, and hung up.

"Another dissatisfied customer?" Reece asked, consulting a folder and shoving the drawer home. His blue, blue eyes twinkled at her momentarily.

Reaching for her phone messages, Maxey yawned.

"Did you know yawning in other mammals signifies aggression?" Reece drifted closer to give her a whiff of his Paco Rabanne Pour Homme.

This was why she spent as much time working at home as possible. Her cozy little upstairs apartment on Spruce, within walking distance of the office, was equipped with word processor, commercial phone line, and a freezer full of junk food. It was perfect for writing her ombudsman column and feature stories for Jim's weekly newspaper. When she did come to the office, she ran into distracting memories.

Jim had hired Reece when the newspaper was first launched, two and a half years ago. They kept it going all by themselves for the first eight weeks, and then Jim had felt flush enough to add Maxey to the team. She and Reece shook hands and flirted for the first time here in this room, were married a whirlwind five months later, and separated a tornado ten months after that.

Softhearted Jim, unable to decide which of them to lay off during all the unpleasantness, continued to employ both warriors in the hope that one would admit defeat and slink off to another job. Only now Maxey and Reece had settled into a lazy truce, were almost friends—which they'd never been when they were lovers—and though Maxey preferred to keep her wary distance, the newsroom atmosphere was usually placid.

The first thing Maxey had done after the divorce was claim back her maiden name of Burnell. Having to be Maxey Macy was practically grounds for divorce in itself. Jim, à la Popeye, had wanted to call her column "Ax Maxey," but had settled for "Squeaky Wheel." She thought she had more good sense than either man, but that might have been because she got paid for her advice.

She slurped at hot coffee, crossing off messages with a blob-prone ballpoint. Junk call. Junk call. Nuisance call—a teenage pest who kept wanting her to expose the inequities in gym-class grading.

The phone rang. Five times, before Maxey decided the menfolk weren't going to answer it.

Frowning at the soles of Reece's sneakers forming a V on his desktop while he read yesterday's *Regard,* she tucked the receiver into her neck and identified herself.

"Oh, you're just the person I wanted," warbled into her ear. "I need your help. Desperately."

Picturing another senior citizen ankle-deep in electricity, Maxey encouraged with a cautious, "Yes?"

"We get your little paper here on Friday mornings and I always read you first."

"Thank you." Maxey warmed a bit. "What can I do for you?"

"My husband has disappeared."

Inwardly groaning for the time about to be wasted, Maxey said, "I'm not going to be much help to you there. You need the police."

The woman uttered something succinct and crude. "They're no help. None."

"A private detective then. I have no experience tracing missing persons."

"Yes, you do. Last spring you found Amabel."

Pulling yesterday's paper to her, Maxey opened it to her own picture on page two. "Amabel was—is—a French poodle."

"Well, of course, and a person ought to be so much easier to find. Humans have credit cards and dental records and fingerprints."

"I'm sorry," Maxey said. In the grainy photo, her blond hair was gray, her white teeth were gray, and her right nostril was bigger than her left. "You really do need a private invest—"

"Do you know what they charge?" the woman asked. "I don't think I have that kind of money."

Maxey tried to draw a mustache on the gray, sweetly curling upper lip, but the ballpoint pen wouldn't cooperate. "Perhaps you'd qualify for some kind of legal aid, Mrs.—I'm sorry, I didn't get your name."

"Stamp. Rita Stamp. You probably read about me and him in the papers. It happened in Glenwood Springs on Tuesday. What I thought was, you could find him and your pay would be writing a book about it."

Maxey did recall the story. "I'm afraid I don't have time right now to do a book justice, though I appreciate your thinking of me, and I certainly hope your husband turns up. Alive," she added belatedly.

But she was talking to a dial tone. Mrs. Stamp had hung up on her.

All she had done for Amabel was describe her

in a column with a plea for folks to watch for her.
During the next couple of months the *Regard* was
inundated with requests from lost-pet owners
wanting equal time, and Maxey had to print a
polite refusal to handle that kind of problem
again. She certainly wasn't going to locate Mr.
Stamp and have all the deserted wives in Boulder
County camping on her doorstep.

Using the recalcitrant pen as a pointer, she read
below her photograph, automatically searching for
typos:

> *Question. I received a letter saying I've won five mil-
> lion dollars in a Florida sweepstakes. To claim it, I have to
> send this firm—Hartshorn, Bigelow, and Jones—twenty dol-
> lars to cover the cost of drawing up the proper documents
> that will release the money to me. My question is, since they
> made an error and spelled my name "Norma" instead of Nor-
> man, will I still be entitled to the money? N.G., Boulder.*
>
> *Answer. Do not, I repeat, do not send H, B, and
> J twenty, ten, or even one buck. Their phone has been
> disconnected, the Miami Better Business Bureau has a
> fat folder of complaints about them, and Sixty Minutes
> is no doubt planning a ten-minute segment.*

So far, so good. She reached for the coffee mug
without looking and grimaced at the flavor of its
contents.

> *Question. My husband bought some cassettes
> through the mail that were supposed to help him stop*

smoking in thirty days if he played them while he slept.
But the tapes were labeled wrong, and he still smokes
three packs a day. What he got by mistake are for expe-
riencing greater sexual enjoyment. Can we sue the mail-
order company since I got pregnant? C.R., Broomfield.

Answer. You'd have a hard time (sorry about
that) proving the pregnancy was due to the subliminal
message and not just your own irresistible—

The phone again. Maxey gritted her teeth and let it ring five times. "Either of you guys know how to use Mr. Bell's great invention?"

"It's always for you anyway," Reece said.

Jim pounded keys, in a world of his own.

"Five bucks says this call is not for me," Maxey said, daring him.

"Sold." Reece lounged backward, hands interlocked behind his head.

"*Regard.* Maxey Burnell," she snapped at the receiver.

"July two zero," a male voice said with soft precision. "Tell Jim Donovan he's cut his own throat."

"Who is this? Hoffman?" Hoffman free-lanced them political cartoons.

"I'm not kidding, lady."

The line disconnected with a quiet click and began to hum to itself. Maxey recradled the receiver as if it were a hot potato.

"Jim," she shouted, ignoring Reece's fingers beckoning to be paid. "Chalk up one more hate call for yourself. I'm guessing he didn't like this week's issue."

Jim nodded without interest.

Digging his heels into the hardwood floor, Reece walked the chair toward Maxey's desk. "Pay up, sister."

"It wasn't for me." She slapped his reaching hand.

"They didn't ask to talk to anyone else, did they? If they talked to you, it must have been a call for you."

"I've got work to do. Leave me alone."

He swiveled her Week-at-a-Glance to face him. "What muck are we raking this week? Potholes, uh-huh. HUD, good, good. What's this 'decent ass'?" He laughed, swaying his head. "'Decent ass'? How come Jim gives you all the most interesting assignments?"

"That's 'decency ass.' The Decency for Boulder Association. A group of little old ladies of both sexes you are more than welcome to interview in my stead. They want to read all the dirty books so the rest of us don't have to."

Backpedaling to his own desk, Reece picked up his own calendar. "I'll trade you decency ass for this week's city-council meeting."

"Not a chance."

The U.S. mail lady bustled in, shuffling through a sheaf of mail, dark curls bouncing under her safari hat. She was small and tan and looked like she jogged daily before a high-protein breakfast. A constant challenge to Reece, she always ignored him to hand the mail to Jim, usually extracting a rare smile from "the boss man" with a dazzling white one of her own.

"Any letter bombs?" Jim asked her now, taking over the shuffling job.

"You'd get nicer mail if you wrote nicer stories," she said, aiming her pert, starched front at the level of his eyes.

"We wouldn't get *any* mail if we wrote nicer stories," he said. "Because we wouldn't have any readers. Bills. We'd still get bills," he added, tossing four windowed envelopes into the lowest stack tray.

Jim's chair squeaked as he leaned toward the keyboard again, and Lucky—according to her name badge—about-faced and exited without acknowledging Reece's "You come back now, you hear?"

Maxey opened her loose-leaf binder to see what notes needed working up first. The phone rang.

"I'm going home," she said, reaching for it.

"Reporters are supposed to be able to work under pressure," Reece observed. "Thrive on it, enjoy it, seek it out."

"Hello, *Regard.* Maxey speaking."

"I want to speak to Reece Macy." From the woman's tone Maxey could sense she wasn't smiling.

"Mr. Macy isn't here at the moment." She put oversweet syrup in the lie, grinning maliciously at him. "May I help you?"

"Tell him if he doesn't pay his rent by six o'clock

tonight, he's going to have to scrape his personal belongings off the front sidewalk tomorrow."

"I'd be so happy to give him the message. Thank you so much for calling."

Faltering under this unexpected cordiality, the landlady said, "Think nothing of—have a good—bye!"

"I won the lottery?" Reece asked.

"A cranky crank. *You* made someone mad, too."

Before he could puff up into full preen, she told him who.

She didn't go home. The phone drowsed, the office quieted, and Maxey lost herself in writing about the public library's problem with vagrants sleeping in the reading rooms. When she switched off the typewriter and peered around, Reece was gone, and Jim slouched deep in contemplation of a pencil eraser.

Her stomach growled, "Luuunch." Obediently she stood, shutting notebooks, capping pens, tossing back the last of the awful—and no better cold—coffee.

"If I take you home for lunch," Jim said, "could I have some, too?"

It sounded more like Reece than Jim, this bantering and bartering. She nodded, of course, trying to think what the refrigerator had to offer worthy of two people, one of them her boss.

He rose and began compulsively arranging the plastic cover around his terminal.

"I've got some interviews at the courthouse this afternoon," Maxey said, gathering her purse to her chest. "I guess I'll work at home the rest of the day."

Jim gazed around the room as if he were locking up for the weekend instead of for an hour. Waving her ahead of him, he set the "Back at— o'clock" sign in the front door, nudging the hands to one-fifteen. The door dragged across the sill, needing planing for as long as Maxey had worked here and, undoubtedly, years before that.

Their newspaper office was across the street and a block down from the big boys, the *Daily Camera,* on Boulder's downtown pedestrian Pearl Street Mall. Paved with brick and flower beds, lined by shops with names like Banana Republic and Rue Morgue Books, and by ethnic restaurants with as many tables on the sidewalk as inside, the mall enjoyed a reputation for being a fun place to stroll and watch street musicians, acrobats, mimes, and other mall strollers.

Maxey smiled and shook her head at the young man trying to wave her into having a photo made with a mock-up of President Bush. Skirting him, she bumped into Jim, who staggered as if she outweighed him.

"Drunk again?" she asked.

"You're the one who can't walk straight." He shepherded her into a side street.

"How far away did you park?"

"Three more blocks. Unmetered parking."

"Hey, we could have walked to my house by the time we get your car."

"You sure know how to make an environmentalist feel guilty. That's okay—I have some errands to run, too."

Jim's car was a pastel green Volkswagen Bug that looked as if it had spent most of its life parked in a garage. Clean inside and out, as car dealers say. Having sat shut up in the sun all morning, it was sauna hot.

Jim turned into traffic before saying, "What's it all about, Maxey?"

"Um," she answered, still picturing lunch. Soup and salad. Or she might have enough bacon for two BLT sandwiches if hers was mostly L and T.

"We bust our butts all week on one edition, breathe a collective sigh of relief as it hits the stands, and then we masochistically turn right around and start the cycle all over again. Are we making any headway whatsoever? Does anyone give a single damn if we fold our tents tomorrow?" Having delivered this outburst, Jim swallowed and touched his throat as if it hurt.

"We're in a mood of angst, are we?"

"I'm getting too old for this buffalo manure." Jim drove one-handed, massaging the nape of his neck. "Poison-pen letters and phoned death threats aren't fun anymore."

"A vacation. You haven't had any time off for at least two years. Reece and I could handle it for a couple weeks. Well, *I* could. You could go to someplace restful. Disneyland."

"You really think you and Reece could put out two *Regards* in a row without getting sued or killing each other?"

He glanced sideways, mouth twisted by amusement. When he faced front again, Maxey studied his profile. He did need a vacation, she suddenly realized. He was thinner, paler, older, sadder than she remembered from the last time she'd really examined him. At—what, forty?—he still had a fine head of brown and graying hair, a close-cropped beard to match, calm eyes under a smooth brow. But he'd lost the quick, sharp movements of eyes, arms, and legs he'd had the first months she'd worked for him.

For the second time today she found herself remembering how she had come upon her job at the *Regard.* She'd walked out of the sunny street into the dim office, feeling nervy and awkward, making a cold call on a stranger, and the stranger had hailed her like an old friend.

"Boy, am I glad to see you," the bearded man bellowed from across the room. He was bent over at an awkward angle. "Come here, would you?"

Maybe she should come back later, when there

was someone else around. He smiled and motioned with an impatient hand, and she began to pick her way through desks and chairs and tables toward him.

"I got a little problem here," he said, motioning below his waist, and she almost turned and ran right then.

"There's a pair of scissors in that pencil cup." He motioned past himself to the far corner of the far desk. "Cut me loose, huh?"

His T-shirt tail was caught in the platen of his computer printer.

"Dumb, huh?" he said as she went to get the scissors. "I was leaning over it, trying to edit while it typed. Guess the service technician will say it's another case of operator error not covered by warranty."

"You've done this before?" She couldn't help snickering, but he seemed to expect it. He kept on smiling as she hacked at the shirt.

Freed, he backed to his swivel chair and sat, stretching the butchered material to survey the damage. "Expensive shirt," he said. "By the time the printer's fixed."

"Could you use some help?" she blurted, discarding her résumé speech.

"Looks like it, doesn't it? You looking for a job? Here, sit down." He offered a chair with his foot, and she settled into it. "What can you do?"

"I worked at my hometown news office in Ohio five years before coming to Colorado. The last year and a half as a reporter. Before that, I kept the books and baby-sat the editor's kids," she added, without meaning to.

"Oh. That explains your skill at cutting things out."

They smiled at each other for a minute, making judgments.

"The salary will be lousy," he said.

"I'll take it," she said.

Since then, they had worked well together, and worked hard. Jim deserved some quality time off.

Excited at the idea of running the paper while he enjoyed R&R, she bounced forward on the car seat and pointed. "The white Queen Anne two doors from the corner. Looks like you can park right in front."

The Bug buzzed into the curb and died. Jim ducked his head to peer out Maxey's window at the house.

"I should've invited you over for lunch before," she said, opening the door and sliding out. "Never thought you'd care to come, but a body doesn't know till she asks, huh?"

Jim slammed his car door and strolled in Maxey's wake as she jumped up the two steps to the porch. "Isn't this a great place? A swing and a potted fern and everything. My landlady lives here, and I'm above." Shaking out a key, she wound it in the lock of her door. The enclosed stairwell made a straight run up to the second floor. "Watch out, these steps are steep."

Jim's hand clasped her shoulder from behind and she turned, startled. "Maxey, I'm sorry. Can I take a rain check on lunch?"

"You okay?"

He stared so intently past her at the staircase that she twisted to look at it, too. The risers needed sweeping, but not *that* bad.

"You okay?" she repeated.

He massaged his forehead, eyes shut, mouth completely sucked into its whiskery surround. "I'm tired is all. And not very hungry."

"Maybe you're coming down with something. The flu's always going around. Maybe you ought to go home and lie down awhile."

Jim lived alone in a cabin in Boulder Canyon. Earlier this month he and his neighbors had been forced to evacuate for three days while a forest fire raged a few ridges to the west. This week's *Regard* carried his blistering tirade against cigarettes and thoughtless campers.

Retreating a pace, he shoved hands in pants pockets and showed Maxey a pseudo-smile. "I don't have time to waste on naps." Moving onto the porch, he added, "And listen. I do love the *Regard*, and it does have an impact, and maybe I'll take you up on your offer to baby-sit it."

She followed him outside with the vague notion that if he fainted, she could break his fall. "Good. And you listen, Jim. I promise not to do a better job than you would do yourself."

He laughed a real laugh and got into the car.

"Thanks, kiddo. I feel better already." He turned the ignition, and the car trembled, ready to go.

Maxey stepped back on the gritty sidewalk, calling, "See ya," as Jim pulled away.

But she didn't, ever again.

5

It rained that night. Not the pathetic hit and miss that only makes the concrete smell, but a real goose-drownder, as the pioneers used to say. Maxey regained consciousness long enough to appreciate the tapping in her ear, her brass bed being tucked under the eaves of a mansard roof, and then she floated into a dream of cross-country skiing behind a silent snowmobile, pink gown and impossibly long hair billowing behind.

In the morning the rain, too, seemed only a dream. By the time she was up and Levi-ed, the sun had surged out of the eastern plains to suck up every trace of moisture. A fragile string of clouds barged across blue sky as Maxey stuffed an overflowing clothes basket into the trunk of her Toyota, first step in the Saturday-morning laundry ritual.

If she hadn't forgotten the detergent, she'd have been gone before Reece dialed her phone. When it rang, she was about to let the answering machine handle it, her grip on the doorknob closing herself outside.

"Maxey! Pick up the phone," his voice crackled the monitor. "Something awful."

Clutching Tide box to chest, she retraced steps, lifted the receiver. "Hi, Reece?"

"Bad news, Maxey. I can't—"

"Take a deep breath, sweetie. Tell it to me slow."

He sighed. "Jim's dead."

She set the Tide on the counter, clumsily dragged out a bar stool, and eased onto it. "What happened?"

"The police were just here. A car bomb. Early this morning. Bastards. Bastards."

She understood this last did not mean the police. Wiping a hand down her face, she murmured soothing noises, feeling the anger begin to uncoil. She should have suggested a vacation to him weeks ago. Why couldn't the fucks have waited for him to have a vacation?

"They're coming over there," Reece was saying, and she glanced up startled at the left-open front door before realizing the subject, this time, was the police.

"Okay. Okay." She suddenly wanted a cat. A kitten to scoop up and hold beneath her chin—warm and soft and comforting.

"I'll be over in an hour, okay?" Reece said.

She nodded and hung up the phone.

For several useless minutes she wandered around the apartment picking things up and putting them down again. Blinking and sniffing, she poured herself a glass of milk, set it on top of the refrigerator, and walked away. The muffled street traffic reverberated up the stairwell until she strode across and slammed the door.

She hadn't had much experience with death, mostly because she didn't have many friends and relatives to lose to it. Growing up the only child of a single parent in a town the size of a football stadium had never seemed a disadvantage. Whether by heredity or environment, she possessed a streak of hermit for which, right now, she was especially thankful.

The fewer people she knew, the less she'd have to mourn.

Jim, too, had been a loner. It was one of the reasons she liked him so much—because he didn't show much interest in her private life, didn't invite her to parties, didn't tell her his personal problems. If their roles had been reversed today and he were waiting for the police, *he'd* have resented having to grieve for *her*.

Feet shuddered and creaked the stairs and shuffled on the landing outside her door. The knock was three measured beats. The fish-eye peephole made everyone look like the Mafia, but one of these two men had on a policeman's uniform. She put the chain on and let them see a two-inch strip of her.

"Ms. Burnell?" the plainclothes one said, holding up his shield. "Sam Russell, detective with the city police department."

It occurred to her that she had no idea what a real Boulder police badge looked like. Maxey slipped the chain out of its socket and let them in.

She waved at the choice of chairs, and Russell homed in on the overstuffed recliner across the room. He perched on the edge of it, though, twitching his pants legs up as he sat, giving the place a sweeping once-over before concentrating on Maxey. Sliding from the arm of the sofa down to the seat, she waited.

"This is Patrolman Naylor."

Patrolman Naylor grunted as he dug a brown memo pad out of his breast pocket and clicked ballpoint pen into readiness. Young and burly, in a few years he'd have to give up pizzas and desserts.

"Do you know why we're here, Ms. Burnell?" If Boulder employed the good cop/bad cop routine, Sam Russell would have to play the good; his soft, husky voice was a natural for it.

He didn't look like Clint Eastwood or Burt Reynolds or even Ed Asner. He looked like Howie Mandell. Part of it—most of it—was his clothes. The yellow-and-red flowered shirt must have come off a rack at the Honolulu Salvation Army. The mismatching navy-and-black checked slacks were too short. But he had the longest dark eyelashes she'd ever seen on a man.

Struggling to remember the question, she said, "Reece Macy called me half an hour ago."

"Good. I'm sorry to have to bother you now, but I'm sure you are as eager as we are to uncover whoever's responsible. So let's get the routine stuff out of the way first. Where were you from about six yesterday evening until four this morning?"

"Here. Alone. Mostly asleep."

"And you last saw Jim Donovan—"

She told him, seeing again the willing little automobile vibrating at the curb. "I don't know any of the details. Was it his VW?"

"Yes. He apparently drove it home last night at about six and parked in his own driveway as was custom. During the night someone wired an explosive device to the ignition, so that Donovan was killed starting it, about dawn this morning."

Maxey gazed at her interlocking fingers. They were beginning to ache for a typewriter. Jim would have understood that, too.

"We'll offer a reward," she said.

"Give the police a few days on this. A reward might not be necessary." He brushed lint off his pants onto her worn, flowered carpet.

"A *big* reward."

"Any ideas who would have done this?"

Deliberately unclenching her body, Maxey said, "I'm sure Reece must have told you about the letters and calls we get at the *Regard*. Jim, being publisher and managing editor, bore the brunt of them. I had some guy on the phone just yesterday. Maybe it was him."

"Exactly what did he say? Do you tape phone calls?"

"No." She squeezed her eyes shut, trying to remember. "I think he said, 'July two zero. Tell Jim Donovan he's cut his own throat this time.' Then I kind of laughed, and he said, 'I'm not kidding, lady.'"

"You laughed? Why'd you laugh?"

"I thought it was somebody I knew, pulling a practical joke."

"You recognized the voice?" Russell snapped, ready to be angry if she'd been withholding information.

"No. I'd never heard it before."

"Then why—"

"I guess I just didn't want to believe it was a real threat."

He leaned back in the chair, obviously disappointed.

"I'll know the voice if I hear it again."

The room went quiet except for the other policeman's scratchy pen.

Resting elbow on chair arm, chin on hand, and unblinking eyes on Maxey, Russell asked, "Did 'July two zero' mean anything to you?"

She shrugged. "The twentieth was when our last edition came out."

"What about the written threats? Were those saved?"

"I don't know. Did Reece know?" She could feel herself slipping into reporter mode, and she welcomed it. Reasoning out the story would take the edge off her emotions.

"He didn't know. We'll need to search the office. How about Donovan's private life? Girlfriends, boyfriends?"

"He didn't mention anyone. I got the impression he was a loner by choice. His parents live in Arizona—oh, God. Do I have to tell them?"

"It's been taken care of."

Russell reached down to scratch one ankle through the white sock, and sunlight glinted off his dark hair. For a moment Maxey's imagination dressed him in a black tux with snowy-white shirt and gold cuff links. Fantastic.

"We'll keep in touch," he said, standing and twisting to look out the window at her landlady's run-down garage. The trousers were awfully tight across his narrow rump.

Maxey stood up, too. "Have you got a key to the office? And I want to see those poison-pen letters if they're still there. Maybe I'd recognize somebody's handwriting," she claimed, to forestall Russell's refusal.

"I have a key. After we've examined the notes, we'll get input from you and Mr. Macy." He offered her a business card with his phone number in raised gold print.

While his companion, who hadn't said one word, and whose name she'd already forgotten, clumped the steep steps to the street entrance, Russell took one more inventory of her quarters from the limited vantage point of the front-door threshold. Maxey turned around and looked with him.

Plain, narrow, Victorian rooms. A newer half wall and counter dividing the living room and kitchen. Everything reasonably clean. Cheap, eclectic furniture. No paintings, no bric-a-brac, but lots of books. A northern view of mostly alley and other people's houses.

She swiveled back toward him. "What?"

"Very tasteful. Homely."

He probably meant "homey," but either word applied.

Maybe thirty minutes passed. Maxey spent them staring out the window, seeing her immediate future as a series of steps leading to a job at some newspaper office within a fifty-mile radius.

She hadn't asked Reece if he knew how to find her apartment, but apparently he did. His "shave and a haircut" knock was habit, not an indication of his mood.

Their embrace was spontaneous, comforting, and lasted three seconds. She stepped back and pointed at Detective Russell's chair before automatically turning toward the kitchen to get coffee.

"There's got to be at least one more issue of the *Regard*," she called around the partition. "A memorial issue. With a reward offered for information leading to an arrest."

"We'll have to get permission to use the funds out of the bank account. From his heirs. His parents, I assume."

"They'll agree. I'll pay for it myself if I have to." Maxey lowered her voice, coming into the room with mismatched, steaming mugs. "Oh, God. Think of refunding all the subscribers."

Reece folded his lips in on a swallow of coffee. "I'll do the obituary. I've got an idea for a 'this is your life' angle, using quotes from his friends."

"'This is your death,' you mean." She sank onto the couch, mindful of the cup. "I'll write up the murder with a sidebar on poison-pen letters."

"You need more than a sidebar. You could go into it deeper with psychologist's opinions and quotes from public figures who've received threats."

"A handwriting expert. To analyze the notes Jim got." She recognized enthusiasm building and felt guilty about it.

"I don't know. One pseudo-scientific opinion like that might taint the investigation. It might send folks who want to help sniffing along the wrong trail."

"Not if we put a strong disclaimer up front. 'The killer might be like this or he might be nothing like this.'"

The telephone rang, and she set her mug precariously on the sofa arm.

Reece took a stab at smiling as he said, "Are you going to be mad if I don't answer that?"

"We'll let Ernestine get it."

"Ernestine?"

"It seemed like a good name for an answering machine." She raised her hand as Sam Russell's rich baritone began leaving a message.

Before he'd reached the meat of it, Maxey was across the room, tucking the receiver into her shoulder. "Hi. It's the real me."

"Ms. Burnell. I neglected to ask you if you yourself received any threatening mail."

"I get a lot of what I'd call disgruntled. Nothing vicious."

"What about Mr. Macy? Do you know?"

"He's here. I'll ask." Reece was already shaking his head, so she kept talking. "No. Nothing. Did you find Jim's collection?"

"Yes. A rubber-band-ful."

"I want to see them."

"Give us a few days to analyze them and you can stop in at my office."

"Have you got any leads, Detective?" she asked, realizing it was the kind of dumb question that gave reporters a bad name.

"Ma'am," he said, "we're doing our best."

✿   ✿   ✿

Reece helped Maxey do the laundry, and then they had a peanut-butter-sandwich lunch before squaring their shoulders and hiking to the office to face the unpleasantness of putting Jim's affairs in order.

It was one of those cool-breeze, hot-sun, good-to-be-alive days, which made Maxey feel terrible. At the intersection of Spruce and Thirteenth, the Boulderado Hotel brooded with her. Everything and everyone else seemed cheerfully out of sync.

The photographer with the full-sized cardboard cutout of President Bush was on the same corner that he'd occupied yesterday when Maxey had been walking with Jim. Irrationally she wanted to acknowledge his come-on wave by raising one rude finger.

Instead she surprised Reece by taking his hand and not letting go till he needed it to unlock the *Regard* office door.

They peered around the room as if it were unfamiliar territory. Reece strolled to Jim's desk and sat so carefully in the oak chair that it didn't squeak. After a few moments of watching him open drawers, stir their contents, and close them, Maxey tripped the computer switch and began scrolling screens.

"Jim already had several stories in here," she said. "A couple pages' worth or more."

"Good. He must have typed up all his notes, because there aren't any in his desk."

Jim's old-fashioned spindle was uncharacteristically bare. Maxey plunged a hand into the lowest stack tray. Bills. She flipped ahead through his calendar. Dentist. Rotary meeting. One entry looked like *Moe to vet.*

Reversing pages, she looked at the past week. It was almost empty of appointments, certainly empty of any sinister-sounding ones. Sighing, she went to her own desk and began making a list of people to interview. She'd written four names and phone numbers when her subconscious flashed a cue card.

"Did Jim have a dog?" she asked the quiet room.

"Mmm, never mentioned it." Reece was busy making his own list.

"There's a note on his calendar. 'Moe to vet.'"

"Hmmm," he said without interest.

"We better go see."

"Go see?"

"We can't let the poor thing starve to death."

"The police probably picked it up."

"Well, that's as bad. We can't let Jim's pet go to the pound. You need a dog, right?"

"Not allowed at my place." Reece finally glanced up, in time to witness her expression waver between zeal and dismay. "Don't you like dogs?"

"Not much," she said. "All that slobber and clicking toenails."

"Maybe Moe isn't a dog. Maybe you'll find yourself the lucky foster owner of a pony. Or a boa constrictor."

Maxey dropped her pen and stood up. "Let's go see."

6

The recorder was voice-activated. In his bedroom base of operations Grady watched the tape start and stop to the rhythm of Josie bumping around number twelve, readying the room for its next occupant and humming to herself.

To give the equipment a more rigorous workout, he went around to twelve with a light bulb that the bedside lamp didn't need. By now Josie's vocalizing had increased in enthusiasm to include words, the last of which ended in several *e*'s when she pivoted and found Grady behind her. Holding up the bulb with appropriate gestures, he skirted the bare mattress and da-dum-da-dummed a few bars of the "Pink Panther Theme".

Reaching under the lampshade, he muttered, "Josie." A little louder: "Josie."

He turned around enough to see that she'd gone outside to the cart with a mound of used towels.

Grady cleared his throat. "Testing, one, two, and whatever comes next."

Dropping light bulb into breast pocket, he made for the bathroom. Shutting the door, he ran water in the basin, recited, "One, two, three," shut off the faucet, and opened the door.

When he listened for Josie, she was still outside, rummaging through the cart. Sitting on the commode, he said, "Tomorrow. We'll do the job tomorrow, Bugsy." With his face tipped into his shirtfront, hands on knees, elbows cocked, he continued, "The safe's a tin-can cinch." Staring between his knees at the sudsy blue water, he snarled, "All right, you dirty rats."

Josie shrieked, and Grady stood up so fast the seat rattled.

She was doubled over in the middle of the bedroom, shaking and gasping. Not from fear, not from embarrassment. From laughter.

Reece had a key to Jim's kitchen door, which Jim had given him before going on a business trip, "in case of emergency."

As Reece's macho little Fiat buzzed along the twisting, climbing highway a tad faster than Maxey liked, Reece wondered out loud if he would recognize the place.

"I can't help you. I've never been there," she said.

Boulder Creek tumbled a few yards from the shoulder, throwing sparks of sunlight at their eyes. The car swooped around a blind curve, and Maxey had a fleeting impression of party streamers before she realized that the shiny yellow plastic festooning the scenery ahead was police barricade.

Braking, Reece eased across the other lane and into the chute of gravel driveway. The green plank house on the other side of the creek was not much more than a cabin. The access bridge, a flat log floor with no side rail, rattled under their tires. Just the other side Reece pulled up the emergency brake and let the motor stall.

Jim obviously hadn't had the time or desire to landscape. The yard was strictly "Xeriscape," all native bushes and weeds and rocks. What trees there were, evergreens and cottonwoods, overhung the cabin from behind, and they in turn were over-hung by the rusty cliffs of Boulder Canyon.

The driveway had once made a loop in front of the house. Now its symmetry was interrupted by a gaping hollow the color and shape of a giant's campfire. Around this grim emptiness, the police department's yellow ribbons crackled in the wind.

"I don't hear any barking," Reece said.

"Maybe Moe was with Jim when—" She faltered and swallowed.

He snapped his door ajar. "Come on, let's get this over with."

The gravel was haphazard and sparse, more like a wash than a pathway, making them watch their feet. They skirted the plastic barricade. Whatever was left of the Volkswagen had been towed away, leaving only shrapnel for Maxey to try not to see.

She stared numbly at the cabin wall's blistering green paint. Both front windows had been boarded over. What must have been a colorful mass of flowers in a clay pot by the front step was now a snarl of brown stems in a broken container.

Reece stepped onto the concrete slab that served as front porch and fumbled with the key.

"Wait a minute. You better knock first," Maxey said. "There might still be police around." Reece banged on the door and they waited, listening. She shrugged. "Guess they're done and gone."

Unlocking and easing the door inward, Reece stepped back and motioned Maxey ahead of him.

She stuck her head inside. "Moe? Here, Moe."

No patter of paws acknowledged this.

"Whistle," she commanded Reece, drawing sideways to give him room. He clamped lower lip with upper teeth in an impressive show of whistling virtuosity.

When nothing answered or moved, Maxey fingertipped the door wide and crossed the threshold.

"Look for a water dish," she said. "Or, hey, maybe an aquarium."

"I'm going to walk around to the back. Moe could be an outdoors animal."

So Reece wasn't present when Maxey found the woman on the bed.

Maxey wasn't a screamer, though she had to stop

a moment in the bedroom doorway, with her hand to her mouth, and take a couple of deep breaths. The woman was sprawled on her stomach crossways on the mattress, face turned aside.

"Hello? Excuse me?" Maxey tried. She rapped on the door frame.

Nothing twitched.

From this distance Maxey couldn't see anything as ominous as blood. Feeling wimpy, she hesitated, giving the room a quick survey: knotty-pine walls, high oblong windows, a closet door draped in Jim's jeans and pajamas, bare wood floor surrounding one little throw-rug island, two chests of drawers and a bedside table, one crazy-quilted bed, and one female body.

The woman's denim skirt sported a designer label on the hip pocket, the white shirt draped her narrow back like silk, and the cordovan loafers, capsized on the rug below her toes, had not come from a bargain basement.

Reluctantly Maxey walked into the room and around the bed, craning to see the face under the salon permanent. Leaning over the woman's humped shoulder, she peered down at a few square inches of visible cheek and one closed eye. A thin black wire tracked across the cheek and into the silver-blond hair at ear level.

"What's going on?" Reece said from the doorway, making Maxey lose her balance and catch herself on the most convenient handhold—the woman's shoulder.

It was warm, Maxey noticed, just as the eye flew open, followed immediately by the mouth. The woman's shriek caromed around the wooden room and bruised Maxey's eardrums.

"Who are you?" the woman shouted as if Maxey were in the next room. She rolled to sit up.

Maxey pointed at her own ear to remind the woman of the earphone in hers.

"Who the hell are you?" The woman's tone was more angry than frightened this time. The earphones emitted tinny chords as she dropped them onto the bed with their transistor radio.

"Sorry to scare you," Maxey said. "But damn, you scared me. I thought you were dead. We're Jim's employees, Maxey Burnell and Reece Macy. And you are . . .?"

The woman curled around, tucking her legs underneath the skirt. "Tessa Donovan. Jim's wife."

People's mouths do drop open in surprise, Maxey discovered when she turned to look at Reece.

"Jim was married?" he said.

Tessa glared at him. "We've been separated the last six years. I live in Albuquerque. I'm in real estate."

"I seeee," Reece said, drawing out the word like he didn't really.

Well, Maxey did see. The woman was obviously not the immaterial kind. Not the type to hum happily while washing dishes by hand in a tiny kitchen with a creek view that hadn't changed in thousands of years. Or to welcome home an empty-handed husband after his long day at a job that bordered on unpaid volunteer.

"Now." Tessa folded her arms with an air of bringing the meeting to order. "What are you doing here?"

Maxey knew how to fold her arms and look severe, too. "We came to look for Moe."

"Moe?"

"Jim's pet," Reece said.

"Oh, the cat."

A cat. Maxey glanced around the floor expectantly.

"I took him to the pound," Tessa said, waving a dismissive hand.

"You don't like cats." Maxey added this to the growing profile of Tessa Donovan's shortcomings.

"Not enough to transport him all the way home with me. Is there anything else you needed? Because I have a lot to do, arrangements to make. I didn't mean to waste time taking a nap just now."

"When did you come up to Boulder?" Maxey had to ask. Tessa seemed like the type of woman who could drive a bargain, close a deal, or plant a bomb as well as any man could.

"Late this morning."

"I guess you've been making funeral arrangements," Reece said. "A memorial service."

"There won't be any memorial service. Jim didn't like fusses."

"Did you discuss this with Jim's parents?"
Maxey's veneer of civility was worn to the primer.

"I told them, yes," Tessa said, her voice flat and
hard on the "told." "They're both old and frail.
They don't need the hassle of an elaborate
farewell." Scooting to the edge of the bed, she
stretched her legs to shovel on her shoes.

"Mrs. Donovan," Reece began in his earnest-
and-oh-so-reasonable voice. "Maxey and I would
like to publish—"

"The widow has enough on her mind right
now, Reece," Maxey leaped in. "Let's not bother
her with our concerns." She crossed the room to
capture his arm and steer him backward. "If
there's anything we can do, Tessa—" Maxey let
the thought wither as they tramped to the
kitchen and let themselves out.

On the front stoop Reece twitched his elbow
free of her grip and demanded, "What's got into
you?"

"Righteous indignation. Keep walking."

"You didn't like Tessa?"

"Let's just say I've got an aversion to coldwater
trout."

"Nice legs, though. How come you didn't let
me ask her about the memorial issue of the
Regard?"

"Because she wouldn't help us with it and she
might even hinder."

They passed the blackened scene of the crime
and leaned into the mild uphill climb. A shout

behind them, "Hey! Wait a minute," gave them pause, and they turned to find Tessa chasing them up the slope.

She splayed a hand on her chest, panting. "You must have a key to this place. I'd like to have it."

"Oh, yeah," Reece said, jamming fingers into his jeans to search for it.

"You gave it to me, dearie," Maxey said as smooth as buttermilk, and she pulled her own house key out of her pocket to hand to Tessa. Throwing a good-bye over her shoulder, Maxey pushed Reece ahead of her toward the car.

"Why—" He tried to ask.

"There's some reason she doesn't want us to have access to the house," she stage-whispered.

"Maybe because we're strangers and have no business—"

"Some muckraker you are." She gave him one little vindictive shove before opening the car door and dropping into the passenger seat.

"How're you going to get into your apartment, Ms. Smartypants?"

"Ever heard of hiding a duplicate key about the premises? Let's go bail out Moe."

Saturday afternoon was mellowing into Saturday night. By eight o'clock Grady had given out five room keys, none of them to room twelve. Nobody, so far, had looked prosperous or guilty enough.

Cleaning his fingernails with a letter opener,

Grady sat at the office desk and pictured himself in the business section of the *Coloradoan* a few months down the road. LOCAL MOTEL ENTREPRENEUR, the headline would proclaim, OPENS NEWEST IN CHAIN.

The Bronco that muttered to a stop under the portico needed a wash. The woman driver hopped out and strode into the office, hands in the back pockets of her jeans. Her fitted white T-shirt read *This Space for Rent. Inquire Within.* She yawned with all her face and shook her blond-curled head as if to clear it.

"Got a double room?" she said, leaning one tanned arm on the countertop.

"Yes, ma'am." Grady gave her the sign-up sheet, wondering if this was his room-twelve mark. "Been driving far?"

She ignored him, printing the information as if her life depended on it. Beyond her pert profile, a shadow in the Bronco rearranged itself against a pillow on the front passenger window. Whatever luggage they were carrying wasn't visible.

Grady brought up the key to twelve and slapped it on the counter. "Have a nice night."

Three hours later he lay on his bed listening to the tape recorder cycle on and off. "Ohhhh, darlin'!" Long silence. "Yesss, yesss." Long silence. "Mmmm, ahhh, sssss."

What a waste of tape.

Grady needed a video setup. Someday the perfect opportunity for big money was going to drive up to his door, and he wanted to be prepared for it. He stretched sideways to switch on the bedside lamp and began sorting through dog-eared electronics catalogs.

"Ahh, ahh, ahh, eeeeee!"

Here was a classy little closed-circuit TV camera designed to fit in a mannequin's head and pan for shoplifters. Only 2400 bucks.

Soprano laughter. "If your loving wife could only see you now."

The male voice, which had said scarcely a dozen words, now doubled the record with, "You can forget that, Nita. She's same thing as dead right now."

Grady let the catalog slide away as he frowned across at the imperceptively moving tape.

"Want a beer?" the woman asked. Bedsprings squeaked and a pull tab thocked. "You going to stay here or what?"

"I don't know," the man said. "You think this is far enough away to be safe?"

"Sure, for a few days. I'll be back as soon as I can get myself fired." She giggled. "That'll be fun, thumbing my nose at the boss, doing all the outrageous things most employees only dream of."

"Just don't overdo it and call too much attention to yourself."

"Nobody's going to make the connection between us. Relax, Ken, darlin', honey butt, sugar balls. It's all downhill from here."

Blinking at Nita's affectionate epithets, Grady

waited for clarification of the lovers' past or future crime. But the recorder switched off until brutal snoring—Ken's, presumably—activated it in rhythmic intervals.

In the morning Grady lurked inside the office window, instant camera at the ready, longing for a pinhole lens on a remote trip wire so he could get close-ups. He had to be satisfied with four quick shots of the woman throwing a suitcase through the Bronco hatch and one of the man practically running between room twelve and the passenger seat.

The two consulted through that side window for a couple of minutes before she strode toward the office. Grady beat a hasty retreat to the far side of the counter, tucking the camera into the handiest drawer, which was too shallow, and yanking it out to replace it in the second handiest drawer.

The door thumped and she crossed the floor, twirling the room key around a shapely finger.

"Morning," Grady said, smile in place.

She nodded and offered the key, pulling it back as he reached for it. "How much would you charge by the week?"

"The whole week? Um, same price per day less ten percent."

She calculated in her head. "Can we pay it all at once? At the end?"

"Well-ll, I don't know." He rubbed his unshaved

jaw. He smelled what might be a rat or might be a golden opportunity.

"My husband has business in the area. The room is very nice and quite reasonable."

What Grady smelled now was her heady perfume as she leaned closer to wheedle. "How about writing up half the bill now and the rest when we leave? You ought to be glad to have two good customers."

"I guess so," he said, fighting to keep a straight face. Maybe he could lease some video equipment.

7

A *July Sunday in* Boulder, Colorado. A day for hiking in the foothills, shopping on Pearl Street Mall, lying in a lawn chair tempting a sunburn.

Not in the mood for any of these pursuits, Maxey put on her favorite jeans and pin-striped shirt and jogged to the *Regard* office. Sliding her key into the brass lock, she thought of how many times Jim had performed this act of faith—open the door, work all day, lock the door, go home. Commonplace. Monotonous. Precious.

"Hi," Reece said. "You couldn't stay away either."

He was using her desk, his being its usual multi-layered mess. Thursday's *Regard* lay open under

his elbows, several headlines highlighted in fluorescent green. Instead of relinquishing anything,
he hooked his vacant rolling chair with his foot and
propelled it toward her.

"What's this?" She ignored the chair and
perched on the desktop, leaning to tap the marked
paper.

"The stories I want to follow up on. To see if I
can find a motive for Jim's killing."

"Hold on there, partner. I get to choose what I
want to check out, too."

"Sure. I'll take the first half of the paper and you
can have the other half."

"The hell you say. The second half is mostly want
ads."

"Yeah, so, they could be the answer. Someone
wanted Jim dead, didn't they?"

She jerked open a drawer, found her own copy
of the July 20 issue and a yellow highlighter, and
stalked to Jim's desk to work.

"How's Moe?" Reece asked, turning the page
and fighting it flat.

"He's a real pussycat." She uncapped the marker
with her teeth and underlined three names on the
first page.

Moe had turned out to be a middle-aged,
neutered male, gray and white, with yellow eyes
and a potbelly. He'd greeted Maxey like a long-lost
friend, complaining bitterly to her about the animal-
shelter accommodations, ingratiating himself by
rubbing his face on her.

"Why do you think Jim called him Moe?" she'd asked on the drive home.

"Because he doesn't look like Curly or Larry," was Reece's smart-alecky answer.

Maxey squeaked the highlighter across another name to investigate and turned the page. Her photograph smiled up, a serenely ignorant Maxey frozen in the past, before the road of life had acquired serious potholes.

She reread the questions/answers of her column. Did the Florida sweepstakes flimflammers have anything to do with Jim's murder? Or the oversexed passive-learning husband?

No. If any of those people were angry, it wasn't Jim they blamed.

She turned the page. Here was Jim's editorial about the fire in Boulder Canyon: . . . *give a fool a match and it's ready, aim, fire . . . was it arson, was it accident, and does it matter to the homeless . . . the irresponsible responsible parties should be spitted over a slow-burning . . .*

"Inflammatory writing," Reece said, leaning over her shoulder. "I already marked it."

"Look, if we can't cooperate here, how can we expect to put out a readable issue of the *Regard* this week? What we need to do is make a list of possibly relevant articles and each of us take half."

"Right as always, Ms. Burnell. No, no, I agree," he added as she rounded on him, sensing sarcasm.

The list took an hour and two single-spaced typed pages to complete, and even then, Maxey worried, they had left out articles and advertisements that might have some bearing, leads they would have to come back to if the first line of inquiry yielded nothing.

She'd talked Reece into giving her the fire editorial. That was where she'd begin, and she could do it today, because fire fighters never lock up for Sundays.

"Sugarloaf Fire Protection," a nasal male voice answered on the first ring.

"Hi. This is Maxey Burnell of the *Regard*. I'd like to know whether the cause of the Boulder Canyon fire has been determined."

"Uh, you better talk to the lieutenant." A hand smothered the mouthpiece but not well enough. She heard, "Hey, Dave, come talk to this fox from the Guard."

"Help you?" a deeper voice offered.

"I'm wanting to establish the official cause of the fire up there earlier this month." She wouldn't correct the National Guard identification unless challenged—it might get her more information.

He didn't sound worried or too interested. "Campfire out of control."

"Name and address of the responsible party?"

"Lord, I don't know. Just a minute."

The phone clinked down. In the background two voices argued about whether Denver could or could not support a baseball franchise. A metal drawer slammed.

"Shizuko Togawa."

"I beg your pardon?" Her ballpoint continued to hover over the scratch pad.

"Japanese guy." He spelled the name. "Address is Tokyo. You want it?"

"You sure it was him?" Maxey said, doubt corrugating her brow.

"Him and his wife. They were so humiliated by their carelessness, it was all we could do to prevent him from falling on his pocketknife. They flew back to Japan the next morning and mailed the county a cashier's check for ten thousand dollars."

"My God."

"Yeah. Anything else you need?"

"Nothing, thanks."

Which, of course, was a lie. She needed a new suspect in Jim's murder.

Rita Stamp sat on a rust-streaked, yellow metal lawn chair in the shadow of her house and shelled peas for the freezer. Her daughter Janice and son-in-law Bertie lounged on the grass in the sun, looking bored but not offering to help. Bertie took time out from throwing green plums at the garage to peel off his Jimi Hendrix T-shirt. As if his pasty skin would do anything but burn, Rita thought.

Alf wandered across the yard, his tongue lolling and his ginger eyes rimmed with wary white. Bertie snapped fingers and whistled, and the retriever came close enough to have his ears scratched before turning listlessly away and throwing himself down by Rita's crossed ankles.

"Ol' Alf misses Dad more than you do," Janice said.

Rita sniffed, burst the next green pod, and raked the peas loose with a blunt thumbnail.

"How long before they call him legally dead?" Bertie topped Janice's remark in tactlessness.

"You aren't in his will, so just shut up," Rita said.

"Dad made out a will?" This was Janice again, practically calling her mother a liar.

Well, Rita wasn't a liar. Jerald could very well have written up a will sometime and not told her. She wrenched the next pea pod open and said nothing.

"Wish he hadn't sold off his gun collection," Bertie grumbled, breaking off a dandelion and methodically shredding it. "There was some things in it I'd love to've had."

Rita dropped her empty hands into the pea-lined pan and glared at the young people. It crossed her mind they both could use haircuts and shaves.

"Don't talk about him like he's dead. He's not dead. He's lost his memory. He'll be back someday."

She blinked fiercely at the pan. He'd better come back and help her eat these peas. She hated peas.

The second most promising July 20 story on Maxcy's share of the list was Jim's biased reportage of the new Colorado legislation protecting hunters from intentional harassment by antihunters.

> *It is now a misdemeanor* [Jim had written] *to honk a horn, yell, throw rocks, or otherwise warn wildlife that a gunman is afield. The National Rifle Association lobbied vigorously to pass this law protecting the right of man to snuff animal. NRA spokesman Rod Mullenberger declined to say how many hundreds of dollars the group spent to assure passage of the bill. Whatever the sum, it gives a whole new meaning to the term "hush money."*

Maxey scratched her scalp with the back end of her pen and reached for Jim's Rolodex, where he'd kept names and phone numbers of his sundry contacts. Under *N*, she found "NRA" and Mullenberger's metro number. She paused to think how to proceed, gazing across the room at Reece, who'd fallen asleep over his folded arms on her usurped desk.

Pulling the phone closer, she dialed.

"'Lo?" a child's voice answered.

"May I please speak to Mr. Mullenberger?"

"Dad!" the kid screamed into her ear. "He's coming,"

was said more quietly. Hard breathing indicated he or she was waiting with Maxey.

"Are you having a nice summer?" Maxey asked.

"Yes. I got some fireworks."

"Really?" And toy pistols and GI Joes and other good stuff, she bet.

"Hello," a different little voice said.

"Hello, I'm calling for Rod Mullenberger."

"This is his wife. Could I help you?"

"I'm writing an article for *Soldier of Fortune*. I'd like to set up an appointment to interview Mr. Mullenberger."

"Okay. How about next Wednesday? Sometime in the afternoon."

"Fine, but can't I just talk to—"

"Twenty-five-eleven Flatiron Way."

Maxey scribbled it across her scratch pad. "What city?"

"Oh. Boulder. I'll tell him you're coming. Good-bye."

"Don't you want my name?"

The line clicked and began to hum.

Maxey could just imagine this vague-smiled wisp of a woman telling Mullenberger he was supposed to meet "someone" at "sometime" Wednesday afternoon. No wonder the man liked guns. The point was, did he also like bombs?

The motel he owned would have a pool, Grady had decided. And a coffee shop/bar combination.

With a giant aquarium of rare fish, like the one he had seen at a place in Grand Junction. He could bug all the tables.

He lay flat on his bed, hands laced behind his head, listening with half an ear to the inactivity in room twelve. After dickering about the rental of it this morning, the woman—Anita Oakley, if she hadn't made it up—left the man and drove off in the Bronco. At about noon a kid delivered a pizza to the room, and otherwise the day had been uneventful. It looked like more of the same tonight.

Sitting up, Grady switched on the bedside lamp and drew the ad-bloated Sunday *Post* across his lap. *Have you seen this man?* underlined the photo of a crew-cut, middle-aged male Caucasian. *Jerald Stamp of Denver . . . missing since Tuesday . . .* blah, blah, blah . . . *family offers reward of $200 for information leading to . . .*

Grady shook his head. A measly two hundred bucks? They must not want him back very bad. On the other hand, if all a guy had to do was spot this Stamp and make a phone call, it would be easy wages. And a nice contribution to his new motel fund.

Pulling at his lower lip, he pondered the best way to get a better look at the recluse in room twelve.

Swinging off the bed, he tucked in his shirttail, skated his toes into thong sandals, and went to collect a couple of bath towels out of the clean linens.

The night was soft and cool and shimmery with streetlights and stars. He scuffed along the sidewalk wondering if he should have brought the crowbar this time. The window of number twelve leaked light and the galloping theme of Channel Nine news.

Grady rapped on the door, calling, "Housekeeping."

The TV throttled down, and half a minute later the door cracked open, revealing a man about Grady's size and shape. Dressed in baggy pants and oversized dress shirt, hair a gray Einstein mop, face a road map of chicken-track wrinkles—nope, this wasn't Jerald Stamp.

The old man smiled enough to bare lower teeth that were short a couple. "Well?"

"The lady—Ms. Oakley—asked for a couple extra towels. To wash her hair, I think." Grady held them out till the man took them.

The man mumbled a bit, getting his voice up to volume. " . . . some mistake. She won't be back tonight. Okay if I just put them on the other bed till she comes?"

"Oh, surely. Sorry to bother you, Mr., uhh, Oakley?"

"Oakley," he agreed. "Thank you, young man. I'll see she gets them."

The guy shuffled backward, pushing the door to, nodding and smiling.

Grady shut one eye, thinking, as he strolled home. The old geezer must be dynamite in bed, to snare a looker like that Anita. Filthy rich, was more like it. And definitely up to something.

Grady could almost smell the chlorine in his motel's swimming pool.

8

Monday. *Even the word* is ugly—muhnnday.

Maxey nuzzled deeper into her pillow and would have drifted back to sleep except Moe walked across her head, grumbling about breakfast, and then the phone rang. Pushing the cat off, Maxey fumbled the bedside extension to her ear.

"Good morning, Ms. Burnell. Sam Russell here."

She grunted.

"I wanted to let you know you could see Donovan's hate mail anytime now, though I can't let you take it. It goes into the police report. Maybe Mr. Macy should have a look, too."

"Right. We'll be in sometime today. Have you got any leads yet on the bomb?"

"Turns out it wasn't a bomb."

"What?" She rolled over and up.

"Someone wired a spark plug back to the gas tank."

"Sorry, what?"

"The explosion was caused by a wire from the engine dangling into a path of gasoline under the VW, all the way back to the gas tank. Understand? When Donovan started the car, the spark plug triggered the blast."

"Oh. Could it have been an accident then?" Moe leaped onto the bed again, as graceful as if he weren't fat. She absently stroked his cool fur.

"No accident," Russell said, firm and patient. "It was sabotage to the car. Cold-blooded murder."

"Oh." She slumped, feeling old.

"We'll be in touch."

"Sure."

His voice got soft around the edges. "You okay?"

"I think so. Do you think so? I mean, is there any chance this—nut—will go for me now? Or Reece? I mean, we're the editors of *Regard* now."

"God only knows. I wish I could give you a better answer, but that one's the truth. It wouldn't hurt to watch your back, for sure."

She was thinking that if she asked the wrong person the right question about the July 20 issue, she'd have to watch more than her back.

"Maxey? Listen, we're also checking out the personal angle. Donovan may have had a friend or loved one out to get him for some reason. Now, don't take this the wrong way, but think about it carefully before you answer. Did Reece Macy get along one hundred percent with Donovan?"

"Of—"

"Think about it."

She pinched the bridge of her nose, eyes shut, and pictured the two men, easygoing Reece and alert, decisive Jim. Neither of them the kind to yell or carry on. No disagreements more serious than what brand of beer to buy for the first annual company picnic, which they'd celebrated at their desks, with hot dogs from the mall vendor—

"Maxey, you still there?"

"You told me to think about it," she said. "And the answer's yes, they always got along fine."

"I just want to remind you that Reece and you neither one have an alibi for the time that car was wired. I don't think you did it, because I can't see a motive. Macy either. But anything's possible."

"I understand." Maxey was about to hang up on this depressing conversation.

"So on that note, anything possible, how about dinner with me tonight?"

Caught off guard, she said the first thing that came to mind. "I will if you promise to wear different pants."

"So where are you going to dine with the good inspector?" Reece asked when she told him. "Burgers R Us?"

They were at their desks, sorting through their things-to-do-today memos.

"An in with the police force could always come in handy to a journalist," Maxey said, blacking out *Decency Ass* on her calendar and penciling *NRA—Mullenberger* on Wednesday. "Besides, I have to get in good with Sam because I'm a suspect in Jim's murder. You are, too."

"Oh, yeah? What's our motive?"

Not twenty minutes later the answer to that question walked in off the street.

The stranger was as lean and wiry as a teenage boy, but the blue eyes and wide mouth were emphasized with wrinkles from years of smiling or outdoor living or both. His straight blond hair was combed fearlessly back instead of where it would have covered up his knobby temples. When he opened his mouth, Maxey expected the accent to be Australian.

"Ms. Burnell?" His only accent was the wrong one on the first syllable of her name.

"Burn-*ell*, yes," she corrected.

"Leo Crown." He stretched to shake her hand, his grip the right amount of friendly. "And you're Reece Macy?" He repeated the reach and shake. "I'm lucky to find you both here. Hope I don't need an appointment."

Figuring him for a salesman, Maxey folded her arms and tried to look shrewd.

"I'm from All Ways Insurance. Mind if I sit down?"

She held up a staying hand, disappointed that her guess was right. "I'm sorry, but we really are very busy today. All week. We're trying to put out a paper in our editor's absence."

"I know all about that. That's why I'm here. We were Jim Donovan's insurer. Under the circumstances I have to ask you a few questions before we can pay off the policy." He left his hand on the back of the chair he'd pulled forward, waiting for permission.

Reece said, "Oh, sure. Sit down. What do you want to know, Mr. Crown?"

"Call me Leo." He settled into the chair, one narrow ankle perched on the opposite knee. "First off, I assure you this is all just routine, because of the manner of Mr. Donovan's death, which was definitely not routine."

Maxey's mind wandered up irrelevant avenues: Sam Russell could learn a lot from this man about clothes—the gray slacks and quiet plaid shirt and charcoal socks.

"Jim took out the policy about a year ago. Did he ever discuss it with either of you?"

They shook their heads in unison.

"It's a simple contingency policy. The main thing is it pays off Jim's business debts and the mortgage on his home."

"That's great," Maxey said, thinking, uncharitably, how pleased Tessa would be.

"However, settlement could be delayed till the police investigation is complete. I understand that both of you are suspects—not strong suspects, I'm sure—but—"

"Mr. Crown," Maxey cut in. "Will you please ask whatever it is you have to ask?"

He grinned. "Did you kill Jim Donovan, Ms. Burnell?"

She fought to keep her voice from showing her outrage. "No, I did not."

"Did you have any prior knowledge of his pending death?"

"Certainly not."

"Mr. Macy, same questions."

"No and no. Unequivocally no."

"Neither of you had any conversations with Mr. Donovan in which he said he had hired someone to kill him?"

They stared at him, speechless.

"No? No. And neither of you hired anyone to kill him? No? No. Since you are not under oath, this doesn't mean a hell of a lot, but I still have to ask, you understand."

"No, I don't understand!" Maxey stood up and rammed her chair forward into the desk. "Why are you asking us this garbage?"

He leaned to lock eyes with her. "Because beneficiaries can't benefit from a death if they caused it."

She pulled out the chair and sank into it again. "Reece and me?"

Crown made a sweeping motion with both arms, taking in the room and everything in it. "The *Blatant Regard*. Free and clear."

❖   ❖   ❖

They had stories to write, people to interview, photos to take, advertisements to sell. But they sat at their desks accomplishing nothing, stunned by their new gift and burden.

"Had you started looking for another job yet?" Maxey asked Reece.

"I was thinking of moving somewhere way off first."

"New York? Hawaii?"

"Colorado Springs."

"And now?"

"And now I guess I'll hang around here with you a spell. Till one of us cries uncle." He tilted back in his chair and banged his heels onto the desk. It was, after all, his. "God. I can't believe Jim doing this. What gave him the idea, do you suppose? Made him so thoughtful of the future—yours, mine, and the *Regard*'s?"

"We were his family, and it was his baby," Maxey said. She gritted her teeth. "And he'd hate like hell to see us frittering away our time like this." Jumping up from *her* desk, she snagged her purse out of the lower drawer. "I'm going to the police station and look at nasty notes. You're supposed to peruse them, too."

"In other words, you need a ride."

"One of the first things we should budget is an office helper," Maxey said, winding down the window on her side of Reece's stuffy Fiat. "Someone to open mail, take want ads, *answer the phone.*"

"Come on—when you do it so well?"

"A journalism student," Maxey said, "who'll work cheap in exchange for the experience."

"Female. Good-looking. Single. A good cook."

"*I'll* write the advertisement, thanks "

"And cheerful. Someone easy to get along with."

"Oh, shut up."

He tapped impatient fingers on the steering wheel, waiting out a light. "Listen, I don't think it's necessary to mention to Russell about our being Jim's insurance beneficiaries."

Maxey threw up her hands. "First you think I'm a grouch and now you think I'm a fool?"

The police station on Thirty-third Street was cool and quiet. The receptionist sent Maxey and Reece directly to Sam Russell's office, a corner room on the ground floor with a view that was mostly parking lot. The space would have been generous for one desk and adequate for two, but it was cramped with four. Sam's, the only one occupied at the moment, was the plum spot on the far wall, but Maxey thought the privacy screen on two sides made it look too much like a rest-room stall.

Sam waved them over and pointed at a pair of molded plastic chairs. Sliding into one of them, Maxey surreptitiously eyed Sam's baggy, black watch-plaid trousers that didn't quite clash with the lime-and-black polka-dotted shirt. The chair felt like cruel and unusual punishment.

"We've got four letters here," Sam said, sorting them out of a file folder he extracted from a gray metal stack tray. "Donovan thought to save the envelopes, so we know all of them were mailed in the last year. Two in the last month. And those two look like the same handwriting."

He fanned the envelopes flat on his desk, and Maxey leaned to see. The most recently post-marked were pencil-addressed in block letters, and Jim's name was spelled wrong—"Donnavan" on both of them.

"No return addresses of course," Reece said, bending over her shoulder.

"May I?" Maxey reached toward the stack and, getting the nod from Sam, slipped a sheet of yellow tablet paper from the top envelope.

You and your paper suck. You think your so big. Unsigned. The twin envelope held twin stationery and a message that was variation on the theme: *Your going to get yours, Mister Sonofabitch Know-itall. You better watch your ass.*

"Charming," Reece murmured.

The other letters were longer, full of profanity and non sequiturs. One criticized the institution of diplomatic immunity, which Maxey could not recall Jim ever writing about, and the signature was Shawn Cutlery. The other letter covered taxation, meat inspection, potholes, and the pope, and it was signed by Herb Herbert III.

Sam steepled his fingers against his lower lip. "We've determined that Herbert has been in a sanitarium since before the murder, and Cutlery—which is the guy's real name, by the way—moved to California three months ago. We're open to ideas on these others."

"Could we have photocopies?" Maxey asked, picking up the two letters.

"Sure."

She smelled them, held them to the light, ran her fingers lightly over the paper. Then she handed them to Reece, who merely read and reread them to himself.

"I can see we're going to be a big help here," Maxey grumbled.

"We didn't expect anything world-shaking," Sam said.

"Damn," Reece said, tossing the papers onto the desk. "Neither did Jim."

9

Maxey and Reece worked diligently the rest of the day to make up for lost time, flogged by intimations of their own mortality.

Reece hunched over his phone and desk, calling people who'd known Jim best, getting quotes for the memorial profile he was writing.

Looking up University of Colorado in the telephone directory, Maxey found a listing for *psychology*. The woman who answered suggested a Dr. Patricia Bonner as being most likely to know about the poison-pen personality.

A transfer of the call later, Dr. Bonner's soft voice politely asked how she could help Maxey.

"I'm writing an article for the *Blatant Regard*. As you may know, our editor was recently killed—"

"Yes. Shocking. I always enjoyed reading his editorials."

"Jim had received some hostile mail and phone calls. I was wondering if you could describe the type of person who would indulge in that kind of harassment. I want to quote you in the *Regard*."

"I see. Uh-huh. Well, the anonymous-threat maker is usually what's commonly called a 'loser' in his or her social pursuits. Passive. The kind of person who avoids taking initiative and therefore doesn't get promotions or doesn't get dates. So the resentments build. And of course the safe way to alleviate the pain is to harangue some authoritarian figure anonymously."

Maxey could have figured this out for herself. "Is there anything else? Something that distinguishes the poison-pen writer from the general public?"

"Well, there's often severe sexual dysfunction—"

"Good. I mean—" Maxey scribbled a note. "Are they more often men than women?"

"About the same ratio, half and half. We're hampered by a lack of data. Few victims complain to the authorities about hate mail, and those who do seldom get satisfaction. The police and the post office have work with higher priority and more promise of success."

Maxey thanked her and verified the spelling of her name.

Dr. Bonner said, "There's one more thing about people who vent their anger in writing."

Feeling like Sergeant Friday, Maxey said, "What's that?"

"They rarely carry out their threats."

Disappointed, Maxey ended the call and leaned back in her chair. Well, what did she expect? A ray of light to shoot from the handset, along with a positive description of hate-mail mongers as, say, short, hazel-eyed, dark-haired, thirty-year-old, bisexual men?

What next? A handwriting expert? Without much enthusiasm she checked the Yellow Pages under *hand* and found one name under *handwriting analysts.* Kim Oviatt.

Maxey dialed, got an answering machine, left her name and number.

Digging out her government directory, she began to call public officials who might have had experience with threats by mail. Within forty-five minutes she had plenty of material for an article, including a quote from one magistrate to whom the post office had unerringly delivered one letter addressed simply, *Mister Poor Excuse of a Judge.*

"Give you a lift home?" Reece asked.

"Oh, gosh, how'd it get to be five-thirty already?" Maxey's fingers sprinted to the finish line of the page she was typing, and she jumped up, reaching for her purse. "Yeah, if you don't mind, I could use a ride."

"Not going to be late for your big date, are you?" His tone reminded her of grade school and the razzing during recess.

It made her answer in kind. "Just because yoooou don't have a daaate—"

"That's what you think. I have a date. We're going to the library."

"Well, that's the kind of place you have to go when you're broke and can't pay your rent." She slapped off the light and stepped out on the sidewalk.

He locked the door with broad, theatrical gestures, as if it were a magic trick, making Maxey dance with impatience. "Ta-da. Would you like to see it again?"

She took his arm, elevating his shoulder toward his ear, and marched him up the street. "What are you and Ms. Bookworm going to do at the library? Look at the pictures?"

"We're going to use the microfiche reader on old newspapers. To look for other instances where cars have been blown up."

Maxey released his elbow, acutely aware that recess was over.

Sam Russell's cheerful whistling of "Stardust" preceded him up Maxey's stairs, and she swung the door open before he could knock.

"Okay?" he asked, looking down at himself as if he'd forgotten what he was wearing. It was a red polyester shirt, but the black jeans fit very nicely.

"Okay," she said. "How about me?" She considered

it only fair to check. She'd put on a denim shirt-waist dress, thinking that faded navy wouldn't clash with whatever he arrived wearing.

"Sure," he said, without a trace of flattery. "I didn't remember you having a cat." He stopped to stroke Moe, unmindful of the gray hairs that leaped to embrace his pants legs.

"He was Jim's."

"Oh. Yeah? Jeez, if he could only talk, as the saying goes." Sam straightened and tapped his breast pocket. "Say, I hope you don't mind if we combine business with pleasure. There's some photos here I'd like you to look at, and I've got a few questions I forgot to ask earlier."

"No, that's all right." She'd been planning to prize information out of Sam, too.

They went to the Wrangler, a moderately priced barbecue place on Twenty-eighth that served immoderately delicious ribs. Sam asked for a booth and slid in next to Maxey.

"So we can look at these mug shots," he said, laying the photographs out like a hand of solitaire as soon as the waiter had taken their order. "You sure you don't mind doing this during happy hour?" His hand hovered over the table as if to sweep up the pictures if Maxey snarled at him.

"I don't mind. I assume these aren't your Sunday-school class?"

"They're all at-large schmucks with explosives on their records."

She spent a long time on each face, not recognizing any one, but intending to know it if she saw it again. "Nope," she said, leaning back and encountering his hard arm on the seat back. "I don't think I've ever run across any of these ugly customers. Sorry. Only come to think of it, I'm not sorry."

He raked up the photos one-handed, leaving the arm behind her. "So what else did you do today besides talk to the fuzz?"

"We're getting a memorial issue ready, so mostly I worked on that." If this had been a normal date, she would have launched into an animated monologue about Leo Crown and Jim's legacy. Instead she had to clamp her lips on the rim of her water glass and swallow the words.

Sam wasn't a detective for nothing. His next question was, "What will happen to the *Regard?* You got any plans to keep it going?"

She drank more than she wanted, thinking how to answer. "We haven't finalized any plans yet. Reece mentioned he might take a job in Colorado Springs, and I wouldn't want to try publishing without him." She took a mental bow for truthfulness.

Sighing, Sam drawbridged his arm away from her and rested both elbows on the table, fingering his silverware. "Seems like if you own the place free and clear, you might take a shot at running it."

So he was toying with more than the knife and fork. Blushing to be caught, she blustered, "How'd you know about that?"

The arrival of their food gave him an excuse not to answer.

As soon as the waiter hurried away, Maxey laid a hand on Sam's forearm. "You don't really think I'd have killed Jim for the insurance."

He leaned away, chin tucked to chest, in a show of examining her. Relaxing back and picking up a french fry, he said, "Nah. But what do I know?"

Beginning on her own fries, she decided it was her turn to ask questions. "Have you got any *real* leads to pursue? What have you found out about Jim's wife?"

"Wife? Why his wife?"

"Or anyone else in his family or friends that might be involved?"

"Nobody's come to our attention yet. He had no close relatives, apparently. Well liked by his neighbors, though none seem to have known him socially. You haven't thought of a friend we might have missed, have you?"

Shaking her head, Maxey stared into the middle distance, picturing Jim's placid face, failing to imagine it angry or angering. "I guess it was some crazy *Regard* reader."

"We'll keep looking." They chewed companionably for a while before he added, "You want to talk about something else now?"

"Sure." She swallowed coffee. "Where did you grow up and how long have you been a cop and have you ever been married and do you have any children?"

"This is off the record, of course." He twisted to grin at her.

"I don't ever promise that."

"I better be careful then, huh?" He took such a long time to answer that she thought he was going to change the subject. "Well, I grew up in Arizona, been a cop for ten years, never married, and don't think I have any children. How about you?"

"Why should I tell you? I'm sure you have a file on me at the station, right down to the tattoo in my cleavage."

His head came around, eyes swiping her V-neck dress, and she chortled, "Gotcha."

Again, they ate without a word for some time. Maxey appreciated a man who didn't have to fill every silence.

"If you did have a tattoo, what would it be?" he finally asked, reaching for another napkin.

"Most tattoos are too serious and sentimental. How about something Warhol-ish, like a Band-Aid, or a UL stamp of approval?"

She hadn't heard him laugh before, and it was worth the wait—a deep, honest rattle of pleasure. "No, seriously," he said. "I told you all about myself, so now it's your turn."

"You call one lousy run-on sentence 'all' about yourself?"

Maxey straightened. "Okay, then. Let's see—I grew up in Ohio—" She waited for his approval that she was saying this in the right order, and he nodded. "And I've been a reporter for three years."

More nodding. "And you know about my having been married to Reece. Oh, and no kids."

"Relatives around here?" he asked, stabbing coleslaw onto his fork.

"No, nor away either. My parents never wanted any more kids after they had me."

He grinned and shook his head.

"And now they're both dead," she said.

He stopped grinning, but his head still swayed. Maxey took a long drink of ice water. The noise of the restaurant suddenly rushed into her ears, as if two doors had opened. Swinging her eyes sideways, she caught Sam watching her, and she gave him a seductive smile, hoping she didn't have barbecue sauce on her chin.

Tipping his face toward her shoulder, he murmured, "So what do you want to do after dessert?"

In case the question came up, Maxey had composed and rehearsed an answer earlier, not expecting to use it with honest regret. "I ought to go straight home," she said. "Tomorrow's an especially busy day at the office."

Sam drew back, sat upright, and shrugged. "Whatever."

A vision of herself at the kitchen table typing *Chapter One* skidded through Maxey's mind. She put her hand on Sam's wrist. "I said I 'ought' to go home. I'm open to suggestions."

He pulled at his lower lip, eyeing her as if she'd been arrested and it was his job to get a confession.

She felt her stomach twist with a pleasure that had nothing to do with barbecued ribs.

Making up his mind about something, he grinned and lightly punched her shoulder. "You want to go over to Crossroads Mall and help me pick out a new suit?"

For the second time that day Rita Stamp's telephone rang and no one was on the line.

"Jerald?" she cried, even as she heard the dial tone.

Slapping the receiver home, she went back to her mending. Her eyes and hands repaired the seam in her white peasant blouse while her ears waited for the phantom caller. Perhaps her husband was a prisoner somewhere, trying to call home, having to hang up in a hurry because someone was coming. She bit off thread, laid the blouse aside, and fished in the basket for the next garment.

She ought to tell the police about the calls. They'd say, "Thank you," in that quiet, bored way, and probably not even write it down. Her hands spread Jerald's blue-and-white tattersall shirt across her knees. It needed a button. After a moment of motionless contemplation she took a two-fisted hold of the tail and ripped it up the center of the back.

❃   ❃   ❃

"You really like this?" Sam said, staring into the three-way mirror.

The salesman hovered, measuring tape in hand, while Maxey studied the gray-on-gray striped suit. She closed one eye, pretending indecision. Lean and relaxed, Sam could have been the centerfold in *Gentlemen's Quarterly*.

"I really like it."

"Pick me out a couple shirts to go with it," he said, shrugging out of the jacket and slinging it over his shoulder like a politician.

Later, strolling through the mall with Sam's purchases and chocolate-chip ice-cream cones, Maxey said, "You aren't color-blind, are you?"

"Huh-uh. Just the youngest of seven boys. Shirts that matched pants and all a good fit weren't a priority by the time I came along. I was lucky to get a new pair of socks all to myself."

"Seven boys! Any sisters?"

"One."

"One! The poor kid."

"Yeah, it was like those amazing animal stories, where a mouse is nursed by a cat and grows up thinking he's feline. Andrea grew up thinking she was a boy."

"Do any of your siblings live around here?"

"The closest one's in Steamboat Springs. We're scattered all over the country since the folks died."

"A big family must have been wonderful," Maxey said around the last bite of cone. "I didn't even have two parents. My dad didn't care for married life and left us to go finish his childhood driving race cars in California."

Wiping his hands with the Häagen-Dazs napkin, Sam draped one arm over her shoulders. "And here I was always envying the only child who didn't have to share toys or snacks or Mom's attention."

"Actually it wasn't so bad. It made me grow up emotionally independent."

"Everybody needs somebody sometime," Sam said, hugging her closer and giving her *that look* again.

As an antidote to the way it made her feel, Maxey forced herself to swallow the truth: There must be something wrong with him or some other woman would have married him by now.

For someone in town on business, Ken Oakley was being mighty inactive, thought Grady. No phone calls in or out. No trips outside the room except a stroll up the highway to the Barclay Bar at lunch and supper.

Grady watched him coming back from the latter. Strolling along the graveled shoulder, head down, hands jammed in the pockets of shapeless trousers, Oakley began to limp, as if his arthritis had just kicked in. A Jeep-load of hair-whipping girls went by him, and he twitched around to look.

Grady shook his head. Horny old goat.

When it became apparent that Oakley was making for the office, Grady scurried behind the counter and tried to appear busy. The outer door clapped open and shut.

"Evening," Oakley said.

"Help you?"

"Is there somewhere close and cheap I can rent a car?"

"Let's see. Couple places." Grady drew the phone book out of its niche. He couldn't resist saying, "Going to get some business taken care of, huh?"

He wished he hadn't, soon as the words were out and the old guy's eyes went flat and cold.

"Your business and none of mine," Grady stammered, flipping through the Yellow Pages. "National is probably closest." He turned the book around toward Oakley, who studied it with the aid of a dirty fingernail.

"Let's try this one—Bargain Rent-it." Oakley's voice was mild and polite. Grady felt as if he'd just seen a rattler uncoil and glide away.

On Maxey's block Sam parked his unassuming hardtop Chevy with quick, deft sweeps of the steering wheel.

Cutting the motor, he nodded at the dusty Toyota in front of them. It bore a bumper sticker—*Boulder's Truthmonger: The Blatant Regard*—and a vanity plate—*Maxey.*

"Yours?"

"Good guess. I don't drive it much. I'm scared to drive it now, if you want to know the truth."

"Come on. I'll look it over for you."

He got down on one knee in the quiet street to examine the underside of the chassis. Maxey squatted beside him, hugging her dress around her knees.

"First off, you check for dangling wires. See there's nothing loose hanging down under here. And look for fuse wrapped around the exhaust manifold. The idea behind that is the bomb will go off on the highway when the exhaust heats up, and if the explosion doesn't get you, the accident probably will." He stood up, dusting his hands, and moved to the front. "You want to release the hood?"

A convertible went by, noisy with rock music and teenage revelers.

"Now take a good gander at your engine," Sam said as soon as he could be heard. "You know what dynamite looks like? Usually it will be two, three sticks wired somewhere about here with alligator clips. Follow me? So just check it over every time you go for a spin."

Maxey rubbed her arms. "Is there any danger just raising the hood?"

"Oh, no. Unless the blaster's wired in a pressure-sensitive gizmo on the release latch."

Was this the end of a perfect date, or what? Out loud she said, "I think I'll get a bike."

He slammed the hood and took her arm to walk

her to the porch. That was as far as he walked her; and he didn't try for a good-night kiss.

Maxey hauled herself up the stairs wondering whether that was part of his game plan or whether, not that interested, he just forgot.

10

The memorial issue was going to be a short edition, just six pages. Neither Maxey nor Reece had the time or inclination to solicit ads, and the only regular features they were using were Maxey's column and Reece's "What Can I Do" entertainment listings. By noon Tuesday, they were ready to paste up.

"So how was your date?" Reece asked, unscrewing the top from the rubber cement.

"Informative. How was yours?" Then her voice sharpened on real interest. "Did you learn anything by going through the old newspaper stories on bombings?"

"I learned there weren't any. Not lately anyway. Not around here."

She trimmed a page of print with a satisfying

whump of the paper cutter. "Tomorrow after we deliver to the printer, I'm going to really dig into my list of July twentieth leads."

"You know what we ought to do?" He concentrated on lining up Jim's photo with the layout's right-hand margin for a minute. "We ought to share appointment schedules with each other for the next few weeks."

"You've lost me," she said.

"That's what I mean. We need to keep track of each other so if something happens to one of us, Allah be praised—"

"God forbid," she automatically corrected, and finished the thought. "I'd know who you were talking with and vice versa."

Reece stepped back and tipped his head critically at what he'd done. "Have we got enough black border tape for all around the front page?"

She stirred through the supplies and produced a roll of smiley faces.

"Jim would love it, but the public might not understand," Reece said.

Mail carrier Lucky marched in, threw a rubber-banded bundle on Jim's desk, and left without a word, as if it were all Reece's and Maxey's fault. She held the door going out for Tessa Donovan coming in.

Dressed in pink sweater and slacks, wielding a straw handbag big as a briefcase, she, too, slapped papers on the desk. "I thought you might want Jim's copy of the insurance policy," she said, test-touching the plastic flower on each earlobe.

"Thank you," Maxey said, finding the urge to smack her just as strong as before.

"Want some coffee?" Reece asked, smiling.

Tessa glanced around the cluttered, dusty room and decided, "No."

"I guess you're mad at us for taking this great business opportunity away from you," Maxey said.

Ignoring her, Tessa told Reece she was on her way to the airport "actually." No need for her to hang around here, the police said. She had a two-million-dollar real-estate transaction in the works back home.

"Tessa, what did Jim do for a living when you two were married?" Maxey wondered aloud.

After a quick look at Maxey's expression to gauge in what spirit the question was asked and deciding, apparently, that it was harmless, Tessa answered, "Taught high-school English."

"Oh. Not much more lucrative than running a newspaper."

"It was a struggle, all right. I was just a lowly secretary then. Jim moonlighted at a grocery store and a pizza parlor and a filling station and I forget what all so we could pay the bills."

"Not all those jobs at once, I hope!"

"'Course not." Tessa's guard was slipping under the weight of Maxey's interest. "And none of them paid more than minimum wage, either, but there were fringe benefits sometimes. Like, Jim didn't know how to so much as change a tire before the garage job. *I* had to take care of that kind of thing." She laughed to take the edge off the boast.

"You're good with cars, huh?" Maxey baited.

Tessa's mouth clamped into a thin, disgusted line. It opened long enough to spit out, "I don't know how to blow one up," and then she was marching out the door.

"Way to go, Burnell," Reece said, shaking his head. "Make you an editor and you can't wait to start collecting enemies of your own."

"Let's go out to the cabin tonight and snoop around."

He frowned. "What do you want to do that for?"

"We're reporters. We're supposed to do dumb things like that."

"The police have already looked around. What do you expect to find?"

"I'll know it when I see it."

They took Reece's Fiat again, Maxey lecturing him on how to check it out for explosives. The evening was cooling toward night, and the sweaty asphalt swished under their tires. Boulder Creek hurdled rocks in its race down the mountain. Some furtive animal traversed the side ditch.

They slowed, turned, clattered over the drive-way bridge. The police barrier was gone from around the scorched earth. Reece drove straight through the spot and swept an arc to point the way out before shutting off the motor.

"Do you hear spooky music gradually getting louder?" Reece said, his hand on the door handle.

She listened a moment before she realized he was joking. "Yeah, lots of violins. *Screek, screek, screek.*" Swinging her legs up hill, she hauled herself out of the car.

Reece produced the key that Maxey had tricked Tessa into letting them keep, and it welcomed them into the dim little kitchen.

They wouldn't need the flashlight they'd brought. The electricity was still connected.

"A-ha!" Maxey raised one hand. "Smell that? What do you suppose Tessa has been burning in here?"

"Looks like the toast," Reece said, nudging a wastebasket with the toe of his shoe.

They opened cabinets and drawers, finding half a box of this and a quarter sack of that. Mismatched flatwear. Odds and ends of dishes. Junk.

Reece paused to study a wall calendar magnetized to the refrigerator. "Dentist, doctor, vet, accountant—what a dull routine."

"We should have made him go places with us, fixed him up with dates. Showed him some fun whether he liked it or not," Maxey said.

The hall closets yielded a water heater and a rod of winter clothes. In the bathroom Maxey swept open the medicine chest to reveal one bottle of aspirin and one roll of antacid.

"God. Even his ailments were dull."

They clumped on to the bedroom. Reece went to the closet first and began feeling in pockets. Maxey slid out the nightstand drawer. One three-by-five scratch pad, two pencils, and three pens. Pocket calculator. Dog-eared dictionary. Two brittle sticks of Juicy Fruit gum.

"Not even a condom," she said.

"Maybe Tessa took them all home with her."

Pulling out the scratch pad and one of the pencils, Maxey began to shade the top sheet of paper with the flat of the lead, hoping for indentations of what had been written on the previous page to appear. They did. It read *employ. tax due Mon.*

She tossed it all back in the drawer and moved on to the larger of the two bureaus. Each of the drawers rumbled out empty.

"I thought I'd be scared, doing this," she confided, trying the top drawer of the second chest. "All I am is extremely depressed."

Reece's answer was muffled from deep in Jim's suits.

Maxey riffled through undershirts, boxer shorts, and socks, shut the drawer, and opened the next one. Empty. Another. Empty. The last one. Her eyes prickled with unshed tears as she stared down at a discoloring premier issue of the *Blatant Regard*.

"Hey," Reece said. "Could be he had at least one interesting weekend. This was in a jacket pocket."

It was an airline ticket stub to St. Louis.

"Maybe the police could trace this and find out why he went," Maxey said, peering closer at the open drawer.

Beside the newspaper was a black, five-by-eight notebook. She fished it out and let it fall open near the middle. Jim's handwriting in blue ink trooped down the lined paper in what looked like stanzas of free verse.

"Reece? Did you know Jim wrote poetry?"

"No. Is it any good?" He craned to read over her shoulder. "'Three miles away my friend/Occupies a bed more versatile than she—' Sounds like old Jim had a lot more fun than we're giving him credit for. Ready to give up here?"

She slipped the book into her bag to study later at home and gave the room one more frustrated sweep of her eyes, unwilling to admit that there was nothing here.

"Room twelve, please."

Recognizing Anita Oakley's syrupy voice, Grady listened in on their telephone conversation the old-fashioned way, on the switchboard.

"Hi, lover," she said.

"Well, it's about time," Oakley snapped. "Why didn't you call last night?"

Her voice went from sugar to lemon. "You don't remember agreeing we don't own each other?"

"It wouldn't hurt you to keep me posted. Did you get fired yet?"

Her laugh crackled the line. "Can you believe it? That bastard Del has suddenly got the hots for me. I can't do anything wrong. It's like the more outrageous I talk and act, the more interested he gets."

"Well damn it, do something to attract the foreman's attention. So Del has to let you go."

"That's not all. I got a raise." She giggled, but Oakley was ominously silent. "If I was desperate for this job, I bet nothing would go right."

A car eased into the portico and Grady thought, Oh, darn.

"I'm going stir-crazy here," Oakley was saying. "I rented a car, but I haven't picked it up yet. I thought maybe you'd be back tonight and I wouldn't have to."

"Don't use your credit cards! You didn't, did you?"

"Relax, would you? If you think I'm going to do something dumb, you better drive back here right away."

Two car doors slammed and scurrying feet headed for the office door. Grady doubled over, listening to one last drop of conversation before he had to go. Because the infinity transmitter worked off the inactive phone line, it switched off during an outside call. Whatever he missed now, Grady wasn't going to hear it on tape later.

It didn't help that Oakley's voice dropped just

then to a soft appeal. "I miss you, hon. I'm so lonesome I'm thinking of . . ."

The office door opened. Grady disconnected
carefully and turned around. One pale, perspiring
man with four preschoolers boiling around him
asked for a room.

It took five minutes to sign them into twenty-
nine, the end unit farthest from the office. Two
minutes to do the paperwork and three minutes
to pick up the postcard rack the kids knocked
over.

As their car's engine noise diminished into the
distance, Grady returned to the switchboard and
was pleased to find it still lit up. With an expert
touch he slipped into their dialogue.

" . . . feel about it," Anita was shouting, "you can
go to hell."

"Tomorrow night. That's your deadline," Oakley
said in a way that reminded Grady of the rat-
tlesnake eyes. "If you aren't here by midnight, you
can just forget about coming at all. I can handle
things from here on without you."

She called him names till he hung up. None of
them was "honey butt" or "sugar balls."

It was nine-fifty Wednesday morning when
Maxey finished proofreading the memorial
Regard. She straightened with a hand in the small
of her back and stacked the pages on the table
she'd been using.

"I can drop that at the printer's on my way to see a guy," Reece volunteered. He negotiated the maze of desks to hand her a scrap of computer paper. "There's my schedule today. Mostly interviews with people mentioned in last week's paper."

"Yeah, I'm going to concentrate on that today, too. Wait, and I'll give you some names." She sat down to scribble. "Boy, I hate this. Watching over our shoulders. Don't let anything happen to you, Reece."

"You'd miss me, huh?" His smile was more interested than usual.

"No, I don't want the police to think I did you in for full ownership of the paper." She finished and shook the list at him. "I forgot to tell you that Sam knows about the insurance policy."

"How much exquisitely pleasurable pain did you let him inflict before you blabbed?"

"None. Leo Crown must have told him."

"Gosh. Leo goes for that kind of treatment?"

She balled up the paper he hadn't yet accepted and threw it at him. He stuck it, still crumpled, into his breast pocket, and left.

Drawing the phone closer, she studied the first name on her list of people mentioned in July 20's *Regard*. The Right Reverend John Paul Leyton, who had just raised two thousand dollars for a homeless-shelter fund. Maxey doubted if there was any sex scandal or misuse of funds for personal gain to be dug up here. She'd interviewed Reverend

Leyton: he was eighty-nine years old and living above a friend's garage.

Gouging a ballpoint star beside his name, Maxey looked up at the opening office door. A mountain filled it, stepped through, and said, "Hey, Maxey."

"Hey, Morrie." She imitated the soft, serious voice of the owner of the neighboring Dilly Deli. Smiling, she motioned at the chair beside her desk. "Here to take out a full-page ad?"

"Huh-uh." Instead of sitting down, he loomed across her desk to hand her a pair of sunglasses and then stepped back to wait for her to recognize them.

"Jim's," she said. "What did he do? Leave them at the deli?" The Dilly Deli had been Jim's favorite place to eat lunch because it was cheap, good, and frequented by right-thinkers like himself.

"Yeah. A couple days before . . . before."

She nodded, surprised at how her throat could still close up if she thought, really thought, about Jim. Then her left brain took over. "Which day was it? Friday? Thursday?"

"Mmm. Same day the paper comes out. He brought me a copy."

Thursday. The twentieth.

"Sit down a minute, Morrie, can you?"

Morrie squeezed his thighs with both hands as he settled into the inadequate chair. "I can only stay a minute." He rocked from one hip to the other and winced. "Thank goodness!"

Morrie Lutz was what nineteenth-century bigots would have called high yeller, his round, friendly face as smooth and freckled as a ripe banana. Licensed to teach public school, he had opted to be a businessman instead, and his oft-confided dream was for the Dilly to be chosen by some TV producer the way the New York Delicatessen, a few doors east, had been honored by "Mork and Mindy."

"Was Jim alone for lunch that day?" Maxey asked, tapping the glasses against her mouth.

She was thinking that "July two zero" did not have to refer to the newspaper's publication date. Maybe something else had happened that Thursday—something Jim did or saw or said to someone. Her eyes focused on Morrie, silent with his own musings.

"Think so," he said. "Unless Reece was with him."

"Did he talk to anybody that you recall? You know—get into any big discussion like he liked to do? Argument?"

Again Morrie gave it consideration. "Not unless it was with Reece."

"Reece?"

"Yeah. Over who picks up the check." He grinned his Howdy Doody best. "Sometimes I thought neither one was going to pay me."

After Morrie left, Maxey rose to prop the open glasses around the base of Jim's CRT. A still-life tribute.

✳ ✳ ✳

By noon Maxey had talked to and crossed off nearly all the names on her list of suspects from the July 20 *Regard.* Joining Reverend Leyton as *doubtful—why bother?* were Governor Romer and the kindergarten rock group Who Doggies. The last line of the decimated list said *Jerald Stamp disappearance.*

Maxey leaned back in her chair, recalling that Mrs. Stamp had phoned her. Friday, it must have been. Just hours before Jim had died.

The husband hadn't been found yet, according to the media. It was certainly a weird enough story to involve murder. But the *Regard* had printed only a line or two of objective facts. Nothing that anyone could hate Jim for.

Still, phoning Mrs. Stamp would be a lot easier than phoning the governor. Sighing, Maxey took a fortifying swallow of cold coffee and began to dial.

"Hello!" The woman sounded harried or apprehensive or both.

"Mrs. Stamp? This is Maxey Burnell."

Silence.

Maxey's ego suffered a tweak of disappointment as she had to add, "You know, of the *Regard?*"

"Oh, yes! Am I glad you called. They haven't found Jerald and someone keeps ringing and hanging up and what should I do about his Beer Bellies?"

Maxey couldn't help addressing this last problem first. "Beer bellies?"

"That's his bowling team, and they want to know should they find someone to take his place. Jerald loves to bowl."

"And you've been getting crank phone calls?"

"Two or three a day. No one's ever there, just the dial tone."

"Maybe there's a problem with your line. Have you complained to the phone company?"

"Yes," Mrs. Stamp wailed. "They say it's not their fault. And they said if I don't pay the bill pretty soon, I won't have to worry about unwanted calls."

Shocked, Maxey said, "The phone company said that to you?"

"Not in those exact words. More polite than that. All the utilities are after me. Jerald hadn't paid the bills for the last five or six months, I guess."

Whether the Stamps had anything to do with Jim's death or not, Maxey sensed a news story here. "I'd like to come see you today, Mrs. Stamp. Maybe there's some way I can help."

"Oh, would you? That would be wonderful. I'm just to the end of my tether. My daughter and son-in-law, they're no help. In fact, I'd be better off if they moved to Alaska like they keep claiming they're going to do. If things don't settle down here, maybe I'll move to Alaska myself. You come ahead. I'll tell you how to get here. We live in Denver, you know. It's kind of a long drive for you, but a lot better than if it was Alaska."

Listening to the disjointed directions, Maxey drew herself a map, thinking that if there was, indeed, a story here, she was really going to earn it.

11

Grady picked up the office telephone on the third ring, swallowing a mouthful of bologna sandwich. "'Lo? Come—"

"What's the zoning map look like?"

He swallowed again and cleared his throat. "Uh, well, Mom, it seems there might be some sort of problem."

"What problem?"

"The, uh—zoning board has to—uh—interpret it for us. The map's real—" Grady rolled his eyes. He'd never been very good at extemporaneous lying.

"Real what?" Winnie's snarl froze him like a small animal in a headlight.

"Fuzzy," he said.

"Fuzzy?"

"Bad job of printing."

"I want the answer by this weekend."

"No prob—"

Clank.

Grady swiped hard at his forehead with the napkin, feeling the relief of the critter who'd just avoided being road kill.

Shushing a dutifully barking dog, Rita Stamp answered the door before Maxey could ring.

Despite Rita's less than succinct directions, there'd been no trick to finding the house, an uninspired brick ranch past its prime. The kind of place Realtors tout as a perfect starter home, in a neighborhood of its peers.

Reaching to grip both of Maxey's hands, Rita drew her three steps to the first living-room chair, welcoming her in the low, earnest tones of a funeral director. "So good of you to come. Sit here. Can I get you a Coke or something?" Then, like a drill sergeant, she shouted, "Hush up, Alf!"

She hooked a finger under his collar and walked him through the kitchen archway, trying a different tone of voice. "You hush up now, sweetheart. This nice lady isn't going to steal anything." A door slammed, and Alf hushed.

Rita's monologue preceded her return. "It's Jerald's dog and doesn't mind me very well. You just never realize how many things you don't know how to do till your husband isn't around to do them for you. I had a new marmalade jar this morning that just buffaloed me. I had to mix up some cinnamon sugar instead." By now she was back and lowering herself into a platform rocker across from Maxey.

"Have the police found any clues to his disappearance?" Maxey extracted pen and notebook from her shoulder bag to indicate she was open for business.

"They found his wallet."

"Really! Where?"

"On the bike path next to the river, about a mile west of where he got out of the car. Back the way we'd just come."

"Empty, I suppose?"

"His money was gone and his credit cards." Rita gripped the arms of the chair as if it might pitch her off. "About fifty dollars gone that I could've given the phone company."

"Mrs. Stamp—Rita—you said your husband hadn't paid several bills. Was that unusual? Excuse me for being direct, but what kind of credit history would you say he had?"

"You might as well ask. The police have been doing it. The same tedious questions over and over. They say they have to look at all possibilities. Like, did he run off on purpose, because of money trouble."

Maxey opened her mouth, but Rita rushed on. "He wouldn't have done that! Left me like that. To worry like this. He wouldn't have. Even if we did owe a lot of places that we couldn't possibly pay right now. Because there's no savings account and my last grocery check bounced."

"You weren't aware of your financial problem before Jerald disappeared?" Maxey asked in a tone meant to sound sympathetic. How could any woman be so blissfully dependent?

"No! I don't know where our money went to. We had some. Not a lot. Enough. Now there's this lawyer calling to ask do I want to proceed with the bankruptcy Jerald had inquired into. How do *I* know?"

"Who is the detective handling your case? Maybe I could find out something new from him."

"They keep changing on me. The last one was something like Pockmark."

"Pockmark?"

"So what can you do for me?" Rita's voice shifted from polite whine to overbearing. "Your paper could run a story about me being in need. People always send lots of gifts and donations to innocent people in trouble they hear about in newspapers and TV. I was offering a two-hundred-dollar reward for information on Jerald, but you don't need to write that, because then folks would think I actually have two hundred dollars."

"Rita, how would you describe your husband? Not physically, I mean his personality."

"Oh, goodness, I don't know. I never had to do that before." She folded her hands and waited for Maxey to give her some clues.

"Quiet? A talker? Serious? A joker?"

"Yes."

"Yes?"

"All that. When he's being a salesman, he'll talk an arm off you and grin till it makes *your* mouth hurt. When he's off work, he might hardly say two words. I always thought he was tired of socializing once he got home. Sometimes he'd get irritated if me or our little girl tried to talk to him. Once he even spanked her for making too much noise, but she was just being a child, you know?" Rita put a hand to her mouth, too late to stop the words. "Don't print that in your story. It sounds like he's mean, and he isn't. Just kind of short-tempered."

"I understand," Maxey said. "What are Jerald's hobbies? Interests? You said he's a bowler?"

"Uh-huh. And he likes fishing. Hunting. Opera."

"Did he camp out when he went fishing or hunting? Is he at home in the outdoors?"

"You sound like the police again. Yes, he's been going on camping trips since he was a Boy Scout. But he didn't run off to be a hermit in one of them caves around Glenwood!"

"Okay, okay. Did you say opera?"

"I hate it, all that caterwauling in some foreign language. But Jerald loves the costumes, the spears and swords and stuff like that. Did I mention his gun collection?"

"No." Jerald was turning out to be a man of many parts. "May I see it?"

"He sold it all off about four months ago."

"Why did he do that?"

Rita shrugged. "Got tired of it. Needed the money worse, I guess."

"Do you know how he spent the money?"

"All I know is *I* never saw it."

"Where or how did he make the sale?"

Surely the police had already tracked down this side avenue. Still, Maxey was beginning to feel the prickle of excitement that usually heralded an important story.

"Some guy in Grand Junction bought most of it. Jerald delivered it over there one Sunday."

"Do you have his name? Any papers from the sale?"

"The police looked through all Jerald's business and didn't find anything about it. It's like they thought I made the whole thing up, but I didn't. Jerald had guns and now he doesn't."

"How about an inventory of what he had? A list?"

Rita shook her head, bored with the topic. "I dug up a photo of Jerald with some of the collection, but then I thought why bother. The police would just throw it in a folder and forget it."

"Well, I'd really like to see it."

It was a color snapshot of a happy man in a Seminole Sam stance, revolver in one hand and an automatic in the other. The wall behind him bristled with rifles and shotguns.

"Could I borrow this? I won't put it in a file folder. I'll take care that you get it back."

"I guess so. If you publish it with my story, be sure to say I don't have the guns. Some punk might decide to steal them. 'Course I do have one that I keep by the bed. Jerald showed me how to use it, but I can't fire it without holding my ears and my eyes."

Picturing this anatomical impossibility, Maxey stood up. "You have a lovely little house here. May I peep into the kitchen and backyard? Have you lived here long?"

Rita scrambled up. "Since our daughter was a baby. Now she's grown and married to a baby of her own." Not giving Maxey time to appreciate that wording, she pushed out onto a concrete patio, where Alf gave one perfunctory woof without uncurling from his nap position. "I do the garden and Jerald does the mowing. Except now of course. Maybe one of your readers will volunteer to mow."

The grass needed watering and weeding, too. There were a few scruffy bushes, one droopy tree, and a tiny vegetable garden that looked as neat as if it had been vacuumed.

"Those nuisance phone calls—when did they begin?" Maxey asked, turning back toward the kitchen, eager to go.

"Sunday night."

"Whoever it is never says anything?"

"Sometimes I hear them hang up, sometimes they've already hung up when I get the receiver to my ear. It's getting so I'm scared they *will* say something. Like maybe it's Jerald's ghost trying to contact me. I read this story once—"

"If you hear Jerald's voice, it will be the real, live man," Maxey asserted. "And then I hope you'll call me."

"You and the police both," Rita grumbled. "But that's the first thing kidnappers say: 'don't contact the authorities if you want to see your loved one again.'"

"Why would anyone kidnap your husband when you don't have money for the ransom?"

"Maybe it was a case of mistaken identity. I saw a movie once—"

"I've taken up enough of your time," Maxey said, retracing steps to the front door, already thinking about her next appointment.

"When you write your article," Rita said, tears suddenly welling up in her eyes, "tell him I miss him something awful."

The president of the Rocky Mountain chapter of the National Rifle Association lived in a house that would have fit right in next door to Rita Stamp's. A bunglow with screened front porch and two concrete ducks in the flower bed. Maxey circled a tricycle parked across the sidewalk approach and, seeing no bell, hammered on the wooden door.

"Come in," a distant voice called.

Feeling vulnerable and intrusive, she opened the screen and crossed the porch to rap on the frame of the next doorway, at the same time shouting, "Hello, it's Maxey Burnell, here to see Mr. Mullenberger."

"End of the hall," came the answer.

She moved into the cool house and paused to get her bearings. Narrow central hall made more narrow by bookcases, tables, bicycles, and the inevitable gun cabinet. As she walked toward the back she glanced into doorways. Living room, dining room, kitchen. All full of furniture, bric-a-brac, toys, stacked magazines, folded laundry, unfolded laundry, *stuff*.

"Mr. Mullenberger?" she called again, almost out of hallway and suspicious that the next doors were bedroom.

"In here."

Pushing the door wider with her fingertips, she leaned to look. The man on the sun-striped bed was wearing pajama bottoms and a welcoming smile.

"Help you?" he said.

Feeling like Little Red Riding Hood, Maxey announced herself one more time. "We had an appointment. Or rather, your wife said to come see you anytime this afternoon. I'm Maxey Burnell. From the *Blatant Regard*."

She doubted his vague wife would have mentioned the *Soldier of Fortune* lie, and now that Maxey had reached the sanctum of Mullenberger's bedroom, she doubted it made any difference what publication she was representing.

"Yes, sure. Come in. Excuse me for not getting up. Sit there." He waved toward a Boston rocker on the far side of the bed.

Picking her way around the clutter of books, clothes, and bedding on the floor, Maxey saw the wheelchair parked in one corner and began to relax.

"Motorcycle accident," Mullenberger said, noticing her noticing. "Fourth of July. Broke both kneecaps, but I'm going to live."

He folded his arms over his pale, bare chest and tipped his head to examine her over the top of wire-framed glasses. Nothing like her expectations, he was young and rangy, too-long hair sticking out at odd angles, wide mouth poised to smile.

She hesitated beside the rocker, realizing this was a waste of time. He was certainly in no condition to be crawling around under cars, rigging explosions.

Suddenly she thought of an entirely different reason to be interviewing Rod Mullenberger. Sitting, she fumbled through her purse and brought out the photo of Jerald Stamp.

"You probably are familiar with the story of the man who disappeared in Glenwood Springs?" she said. "His wife asked me for help. I'm not really sure what I can do, but there are a few leads I was checking. Turns out he's a gun collector."

Mullenberger reached to take the photo she held out and studied it in silence.

"Apparently Jerald Stamp sold his collection

several months ago to someone in Grand Junction," Maxey said. "But there's no written record of it. Can you suggest how we could find out who bought it?"

"Well, first off, it isn't a collection," he said, offering the picture back.

"Those are only a few of what he had."

"No, but if they're representative of his guns, what he had wasn't a collection but an accumulation. There's no pattern to it. A true collector concentrates on a particular field. Like all Kentucky rifles, or all eighteenth-century pistols. It's planned and selective. Here Stamp's got a Colt Frontier handgun and a forty-five automatic, and in the back, there, a Remington 788 rifle, a 600, a Commemorative Winchester twelve-gauge—"

"So this wasn't a valuable collect—uh—accumulation?"

"The individual pieces are valuable, but they wouldn't have interested anyone as a package deal. Not a collector. If someone was just after weapons, any kind of weapons, he might have bought the whole lot."

"A terrorist?" Jerald Stamp's complexity continued to grow.

"Not necessarily. Could be a legitimate gun dealer just adding to his stock. I's you, I'd look in the Grand Junction Yellow Pages under guns and make some exploratory calls."

"Good idea." She put the picture away before

looking him in the eye. "I'm also interested in people who know how to blow up cars."

His social smile straightened into a blank stare. "Your editor. I was very sorry to hear about that."

"I guess your expertise doesn't extend to that kind of firepower. You wouldn't have any advice on how I could track down who killed him."

He felt behind himself to reposition a mashed pillow. "Ms. Burnell, did you know that the NRA trained thousands of soldiers for fighting in World War One, and that in many cases it was the only marksmanship training they received before being shipped overseas? Same thing World War Two, only more so."

"No, I—"

"We're real proud of what we did for our country, and we want to be ready to do it again if the need arises. But there's so many people who like guns, there's bound to be some who like them for the wrong reason. You see what I'm saying?"

"Yes."

"It may turn out to be that Mr. Donovan's killer is proguns, but that doesn't mean he's a killer *because* he's proguns. See what I mean?"

"Yes, of course." She stood, making the rocker dip and dance. "I hope you're out on your own two feet soon," she added with a smile.

"Oh, I will be. Look at this." He raised each stiff leg, one at a time, three inches off the bed.

She knew she was supposed to be impressed, but

she felt depressed instead. "Is there someone around here if you need something?"

"The wife and kids will be back shortly."

"Okay. Well, I appreciate your help."

"Hey, listen, if you have any more questions, just give me a call," he said as she reached the door to the hall. "And hey, listen. Listen!"

She stuck her head back into the room, eyebrows elevated.

"This Stamp guy didn't have"—he stabbed the air with a forefinger—"a *collection*. It was an *accumulation*. But it could also be a *battery*."

"Meaning?"

"Meaning he had them to use. Meaning you ought to watch yourself."

"I'll do that. Thanks."

Halfway to the front door, she heard his shout of, "Anytime you want to learn defensive marksmanship, give us a ring."

12

Back at the office, Maxey phoned every one of the dozen listings under *guns and gun-smiths* in the Grand Junction phone book. None of them knew anything about Jerald Stamp except what they read in the papers.

At four o'clock, Reece came dragging in from an equally exasperating day of following possibilities to their dead ends. He offered to buy Maxey a drink—hell, he'd even splurge for dinner—and she added to his pattern of failures by saying no.

In Fort Collins, old man Oakley must have been experiencing frustration as the deadline approached and Anita did not. Grady listened with him for the

Bronco that didn't come, the phone that didn't ring.

Once, at about ten o'clock, a crash in room twelve made Grady hold his breath, anxious that things were about to be thrown—*his* things—to vent growing anger. But quiet descended again until midnight. Then the IT's high fidelity conveyed the drop of a chain, the rotation of a doorknob. And slipping into the dim office, Grady was in time to see Oakley striding up the road toward the tavern, too mad to limp.

The in memoriam issue of the *Blatant Regard* that went into distribution Thursday looked fine. Maxey was proud of it.

Jim's picture in the upper-right corner was balanced by the boxed reward offer in the lower left. Like Rita, Maxey wasn't sure where the money—five hundred dollars in this case— would come from. But she'd beg, borrow, or steal it—well, at least one of the first two—if it brought Jim's killer to justice and her own peace of mind back.

She punched her ex-husband's biceps as he leaned straight-armed on her desk, studying the front page lying there. "Ready to start on next week's edition?"

"Say you were to buy me out," Reece said. "How much would it be worth to you?"

Hoping he was kidding, she solemnly dug fingers in jeans to bring out a wadded bill and some change.

"Okay, then, I guess I'm ready to start on next week's edition," he grumbled.

Sam Russell phoned while Maxey was opening the mail. She and Reece had flipped a quarter to see who'd go out to peddle advertising, and Reece had lost, ungraciously.

"Hi," she said to Sam, slitting the last envelope and tossing an invoice onto the payables pile. "Leo Crown better give us clear title soon so we can pay our bills. I'd hate to spoil Jim's good record."

"He didn't have any irate creditors, huh?"

"He kept his checkbook neat and current, looks like."

"No big payments in or out that you can't account for?"

"Nope. No blackmail around here." She wriggled deeper into the chair and tipped back to stretch. "Anything new with you?"

"The only fingerprints on the hate notes were Donovan's."

After a moment of nothing but white noise, Maxey prompted, "And?"

"I have to have supper sometime tonight and I hate to eat alone."

She didn't even ask him what he was wearing. "How about Bennigan's at six-thirty?"

The outside door opened, dumping sunlight and

the sounds of traffic into the room. Maxey stuck a finger in her free ear to hear Sam's answer.

"Make it seven and you've got yourself a date."

"Whoa," she said. "I thought that *I* was doing *you* a favor."

Her visitor was a sweet-faced young woman in flower-child garb—a ruffled camisole top and an ankle-length, tie-dyed skirt. Hair in pigtails. Nothing unusual on the Pearl Street Mall, even in the eighties. Maxey smiled and held up a finger to show she'd be only a minute. Nodding, the woman dropped her quilted shoulder bag onto the chair by Maxey's desk and folded her arms on her chest.

Sam was saying, " . . . pick up the check," and Maxey wasn't sure which pronoun had preceded that. What's more, she didn't care.

"See you tonight then," she said, leaning toward the phone cradle.

"See you, Max."

She sighed as she hung up. First his clothes and now his name for her. Why couldn't she find a man who didn't need to be straightened out?

"What can I do for you?" she asked the patiently waiting woman.

"You're Maxey Burnell. You left a message on my answering machine, and I was in the neighborhood anyway, so I thought I'd just stop in and see what you wanted. As long as it isn't advertising you're selling. I'm on a real limited budget."

"Oh, gosh, help me out here," Maxey said, rubbing her forehead. "Your name is?"

"Kim Oviatt." And when Maxey still looked blank, she added, "I'm a musician?" Still, Maxey struggled to remember. "Teach guitar?" Maxey shook her head. "A handwriting analyst?"

"Bingo!" Maxey smiled in comprehension. "Please, forgive me for being such a scatter—sit down won't you?"

"I charge ten dollars for an oral report and twenty for a written," Kim said, staying on her feet until this information could be satisfactorily processed.

"Oh. Well, I'm not authorized to pay anything. I was hoping for an interview. You'd get some free publicity out of it."

The woman's lips thinned in a disapproving line and she stood a little straighter.

"And if your expertise should lead to an arrest, there's a five-hundred-dollar reward."

Kim reached to pick up her purse, but it was only to give her room to sit down. "Okay, I guess. What do you want to know?"

Maxey shuffled papers on the desk, opened and shut drawers, trying to recall where she'd put the photocopy the police had let her make. "I've got a couple threatening notes here someplace. Maybe you could tell me something about the person who wrote them."

"Probably."

"A-ha, here we are." Maxey withdrew the folded sheet of bond paper from the outside pocket of her briefcase. Mashing the creases flat on the desktop, she pushed it over to Kim.

There was a long, motionless, studying silence. Maxey found her own attention wandering to silly schoolgirl stuff, like which lingerie she should wear tonight.

"Well, the first thing I notice is this person is pessimistic. See how the writing runs downhill?" Kim poked at the paper with a pearl-white fingernail.

"Uh-huh."

"Secretive."

"Uh-huh."

"Thrifty. Intelligent."

"Intelligent, huh?"

"Cool, calm, and collected."

"I beg your pardon?" Maxey's surprise sharpened her voice.

"Oh, yes. Very even-tempered."

"How can you say that? What the note says shows he was madder than hell," Maxey said.

"We don't read the words, we analyze the writing. See the crossbars on the *t*'s are most of them curved down like inverted plates? That means self-control. And the cross isn't high or low, but halfway, and that also indicates calm thoughtfulness."

Maxey gritted her teeth. "So we're looking for a solemn, conservative, easygoing sociopath!"

Frowning at the implied criticism of her ability, Kim handed the paper across the desk and picked up her bag. "I guess you don't want to know about the big looped *b*'s," she said, rising.

"What about them?"

"They show kindness and understanding."

Maxey, wearing three-inch heels, clip-clopped up her stairs ahead of Sam Russell. They'd had too much to eat and drink and gone to a movie. Now she was torn between wanting to sleep and wanting to see if Sam's underwear was as gaudy as his outerwear.

Jim's cat welcomed them by blocking the front door and complaining of loneliness. Gently plowing Moe aside with one foot, Maxey flipped on the light and smiled encouragement over her shoulder at Sam, who was compulsively checking the knot of his yellow-and-purple plaid tie.

"Have a seat," she said on her way to the bathroom to do some checking of her own. "I'll be right back."

"Mind if I make us some coffee?" he asked, already in the kitchen.

While she was saying "Go ahead," the phone began to ring. "'S okay. Ernest—my answering machine will get it."

She paused, hand on the bathroom light switch, hearing Rita Stamp's soaring whine. "Maxey. Maxey!"

The shrillness raised goose bumps on Maxey's arms. She strolled back to the living room, in case she had to lift the receiver.

"Well, damn it!" The phone made scuffling

sounds, as if Rita had dropped her end. Then; "I'm sorry, but I just can't take it anymore. What else do I say?"

Silence.

Maxey stared ruefully into Sam's gorgeous eyes as he stood motionless, one scoop of instant coffee poised above a cup. "I guess I better—" she began.

The roar, the explosion, was obscenely loud. One single detonation slamming along the telephone lines into the serenity of Maxey's living room. The sound twitched Maxey like an electric shock and made Sam scatter coffee on the floor.

He beat her to the phone, yanked it up, yelled into it for several fruitless moments. Then he clicked the disconnect, trying for a dial tone.

Slapping handset into cradle, he strode for the door. "It's still off the hook at her end. You know where she lives?"

"Yes, but—"

"Come on. We'll call 911 from my car radio."

"She lives in Denver," Maxey shouted above the clatter of their shoes on the stairs.

"Shit. Okay."

Rita Stamp's unassuming neighborhood was now very assuming with its milling spectators and lights. Sam parked across someone's driveway, and they walked half a block to the barricades. Peering past Sam's shoulder while he conferred with a guard, Maxey noted that lights blazed all over the house—wouldn't the electric company hate that.

Sam took her arm and led her around the sawhorse. "How squeamish are you?"

"I'm a reporter."

"You're that callous, huh? Should be no problem then."

"What do you mean?" She tried to keep up with his stride. "What happened?"

"She's dead. You'll maybe have to identify her."

It wasn't a surprise, but it still felt like a roller-coaster dip.

Sam flashed his badge at a huddle of uniforms on the front porch and hauled Maxey through the front door. "Don't touch anything," he said, craning at the empty living room and kitchen before striking out in the opposite direction, toward voices at the back of an abbreviated hall.

The room was already full of people, all male, mostly dressed in blue. Someone was shouting to "Get the hell out," making an ebbtide at the door that Sam and Maxey had to swim against.

"Greg Cheski?" Sam shouted over heads.

"Yo," was the distant answer.

Following Sam's blocking, Maxey stumbled into the bedroom and froze, hand to mouth, transfixed by the bloody heap of laundry that had been Rita Stamp.

She lay on the bed, one pale leg dangling over the side. Maxey wanted to go draw the terrycloth robe over the flabby, vulnerable thigh, which was an especially inappropriate thought, because Rita's face needed covering more—what was left of it. Maxey averted her own face, fighting down a gagging reflex.

"Hey, Sam! What are you doing in this neck of the woods?" the man who must be Greg greeted them. He was short and squat and had a mustache like a plucked eyebrow.

"Greg." Sam sketched a salute. "I think we're your witnesses in this case. This is Maxey Burnell, who"—Sam pointed at the phone receiver in Rita's twisted lap—"the victim was calling when the shot was fired."

The gun was there, too, Maxey saw now. A few inches away from Rita's slack right hand. A little snub-nosed pistol.

Greg nodded once, acknowledging the introduction. "Relative? Friend?"

"I was trying to help her on a professional basis," Maxey said. By turning sideways, she put poor Rita out of her line of sight. "I'd only talked to her a couple times."

"But this is her? Rita Stamp?" Greg demanded.

Maxey forced herself to look once more, trying to see only the undamaged left side of the face. "Yes."

Sam was prowling around the room, hands clasped behind his back, like an interested patron in a museum. "You think it's murder or suicide?" he asked his colleague.

"Could be either. What did she say on the phone?"

"Look, you guys, could we go sit in the front room to discuss it?" Maxey was ashamed to have to beg.

"Sure," Greg said, spreading his arms to usher them out, the museum curator being a good host.

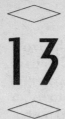

13

"*Is that clock right?*" Maxey punctuated the question with a yawn.

Sam's eyes glittered in the green glow of the dashboard as they sped north on the Boulder Denver Turnpike. "Two forty-eight," he confirmed. "Give or take a few seconds. What's the matter? Past your bedtime?"

She tipped her head back against the seat, shut her eyes, saw Rita's bloody face, and was immediately wide-awake. "God, I don't know how you can stand it, examining dead bodies all the time."

"Yeah, well, I'd much rather examine live ones."

She peeked with one eye at his seeming concentration on the highway. His head started to turn and she shut the eye.

"There was something wrong back there," she said.

He snorted derision. "Oh, you noticed that, did you?"

"No, I mean something subtle. Something was out of place. Or missing."

Sam waited for her to think of it, his fingertips casually steering the hurtling car. Before long she realized her mind had slipped off the trail and was currently mulling over how to write up Rita's death for the next *Regard.* Maybe it would help to think out loud.

"Your friend Greg said there hadn't been a break-in. There was nothing obvious stolen, like the TV. Her handbag was on the bureau with money in it."

Sam didn't even nod, letting her wander on her own.

"That was probably her gun, you know," she said, remembering Rita's description of how she had to fire it with eyes and ears covered. "I didn't think women used guns for suicide."

"Some do."

"But she was scared of guns. Seems like if she were going to kill herself, she'd take a bunch of pills."

"You don't think it's suicide."

There was a long silence. "My left brain thinks it was. My right brain keeps flirting with murder."

"What she said on the phone. Was there any hidden message in that?"

"Hidden message?"

"Yeah. I mean it sounded straightforward enough. She was under a lot of pressure right now. Probably decided her husband was gone for good. End it all, *blam.* Gun right there in the nightstand."

"Why call me?"

"Suicides usually leave notes. This day and age of electronics, it's just as simple to leave one on an answering machine."

"I guess she wanted me to know it really was suicide and not Jerald or her son-in-law or somebody murdering her."

"She should have left a less enigmatic message." Sam dropped the speed out of cruise control and coasted to the Baseline stoplight.

"That was the way she was, though. Kind of flighty and vague. She wouldn't have had the imagination for any secret messages. Poor Rita." After another stoplight, Maxey forced herself to ask, "Sam? If I'd answered the phone instead of letting the answering machine do it—"

"You wouldn't have made one damn bit of difference."

She didn't know whether to be comforted or insulted.

The next day was just one damn thing after another.

It had been almost three-thirty by the time Sam had walked her to the door, not kissed her good night, and left. She'd fallen asleep at once, only to wake an hour later with a headache that hadn't succumbed to two aspirin and an allergy tablet. Giving up, she sat at the dinette table writing an eyewitness account of Rita's death while the memory was still vividly red and white. Moe curled up on her toes, his weight anchoring her to the task.

Once, she gently withdrew her feet and went to replay Ernestine, listening to Rita's anguished voice three times, straining to hear anything new in the words or the hissing background. The fourth go-round, Maxey lip-synced, "What else do I say?" and, switching it off, she muttered, "Not a blasted thing, Rita."

When sunlight washed out the overhead fluorescent, she took a shower, made some toast, considered going back to bed, and didn't.

When she reached the office, Reece was already ensconced at her desk, complaining on the phone to Leo Crown, apparently. "So if it takes another month or two to free our money up, will the insurance company write our creditors a letter of explanation? Damn right you won't. By the time you guys get around to letting us handle our business, there may not be a business left to handle."

Maxey used both hands to wipe a hole in the papers on Reece's desk and sat down to work. He hung up the receiver too hard and without a valediction.

"Hey, Reece, you know what? This is the day that Jim had down for Moe to go to the vet."

"So take him," he said distractedly.

"Where? When? Why?"

Not getting an answer to any of these, Maxey pushed herself up to go to Jim's desk and Rolodex. It was under V, of course—a Dr. Yule Zimmerman. Thankful that she hadn't needed to go through the Yellow Page listings trying every vet from A to Z, Maxey dialed on Jim's phone.

To the woman who answered, she said, "Hi. My name is Maxey Burnell, and I'd like to bring Jim Donovan's cat in for his appointment, but I don't know what time."

There was a wait while a record was looked up. Maxey examined a hangnail, wondering where to get a cat carrier on short notice.

"I'm sorry, but he's not on our appointment book for today," the woman said. "Could you have mistaken the date?"

"Yeah, I guess." Maxey frowned at the calendar in front of her, Jim's clear handwriting smack in the middle of this Friday's block—*Moe to vet.*

"What was the cat—Moe, isn't it? What was Moe coming in for? Is he sick?"

"Oh, no. The appointment was made a couple weeks ago at least, and I don't know—" Maxey searched her meager knowledge of cat physiology. "Was he due for some kind of booster shot maybe?"

There was the sound of shuffling charts. "No,

nothing. He's current on everything till, let's see—October."

"Oh."

"Can you ask Mr. Donovan about it?"

Surprised that there was even one person in the county who didn't know about Jim, Maxey said gently, "No. Moe belongs to me now. Thanks anyway."

Maybe Jim had only intended to make the appointment, but that still didn't explain why he wanted it. Resolving to examine Moe carefully tonight, Maxey put the mystery out of her mind.

The morning was rife with interruptions: sales reps and door-to-door vendors, telephone solicitations and wrong numbers, broken typewriter ribbons, lost notes, an empty coffee jar. Following the natural law of wasted time, the day stretched on forever. At three o'clock, Reece abandoned her, claiming he was going to see a man about some advertising, but going out suspiciously empty-handed.

Finally on her way out the door on the shy side of an eight-hour shift, Maxey paused to answer the phone one last time. "*Regard,*" she snapped.

"Didn't anybody tell you to have a nice day today?"

"Hi, Sam." Her voice warmed.

"It was suicide," he said, getting right to the point. "The gun was hers. It had her fingerprints overlaid on Jerald's, and no one else had touched it or wiped it clean. Angle of bullet entry, powder burns—everything's consistent with her doing it herself."

"Uh-huh. Case closed?"

"All but the paperwork."

"And what's the official word on Jerald?"

"He's probably skipped the country to escape his bad debts."

"And anything new on Jim?"

He huffed a frustrated breath. "What is this, a fucking press conference? I'm going home to get some sleep."

"What's your home phone number?" She set down her bag to pick up a pen and pad.

"Why?"

"In case I think of something in the night."

"Oh? Like what?"

"How the hell would I know now what I'm going to think of in the middle of the night? Come on, Sam, I'm not asking for an arm or a leg. I just want your goddamn number."

"Okay, but it's unlisted. Keep it to yourself."

"Jeesh. Is this why you're still single?" she said, and immediately wished she hadn't.

"Why is that?" He sounded irritable, going on irate.

"Because you're so afraid of getting involved, you won't even let a female have your unlisted number."

"Listen, Max. The reason I'm not married is I've

seen what happens to cops and wives. The divorce rate is over the top. I've never found a woman willing to play second guitar to my job."

"Oh." Her store of snappy comebacks was empty. "Oh."

"If somebody's trying to break in your house or something, call 911."

"Thanks a million."

"If you need anything else, call 344-5876."

"What's that—dial-a-prayer?"

"It's the number you wanted. And Maxey"— his voice glided from high gear into idle—"You're no clinging vine. You're a wall. And honey, that's a compliment."

He hung up on her while her mouth was still open.

Maxey was still thinking about Sam's idea of a compliment as she unlocked her front door. She could hear Moe talking to her when she was halfway up the stairs. Sliding key into lock, she answered in the unnaturally sweet tones of pet owner to pet.

"Okay, okay, here I am. Supper's a jiffy away. Back up so I can get in."

She reached down to haul the cat out of the doorway and had a flashback of Rita making the same movement, talking the same dopey way.

Digging the scrap of paper from her skirt pocket, she went straight to the phone. Of course, Sam wasn't home yet. After his terse, recorded command of "Leave me your message," she said her name and number and hung up. Ignoring Moe's theatrics over not being served his savory sea stew yet, she rewound Ernestine and listened one more time to Rita's last words.

When Sam returned the call, Maxey was stretched out on the couch, sharing a bowl of vanilla ice cream with a no-longer-starving cat.

"What is this—a test of my response time?" Sam said without preamble.

"What happened to the dog?" she said.

"What dog?"

"Rita Stamp's dog. Or to be more exact, Jerald's dog. Alf."

"Is it important?"

"Might be. The day I went to talk to her, he was very defensive, barking all over the place. But there was no sign of him on the night of her death."

"Probably a neighbor took him in, or he ran off."

"He's not barking on the telephone message either."

"Well, he wouldn't, would he, if it was suicide, which it was. Just more corroborating evidence."

"You find out where the dog is, and then I'll agree with you."

"You think someone offed the dog and then offed Rita?" He had a knack for sounding the way her father had when Maxey had been her brattiest.

"Why couldn't that have happened?" She could sound a lot like an exasperated mother herself.

"Because why would the killer go to the trouble to hide the dog's body? Suicides often destroy their pets first. They don't want to leave them homeless."

"Rita didn't care that much about Alf. She did care a lot about herself."

"Listen, Max, it's been nice talking to you, but I gotta get some sleep here."

"Don't call me Max," she said to a dial tone. "And Alf wouldn't have barked at Jerald!" she yelled, as if that would do any good.

Putting the phone aside, she shoveled Moe into her lap again and, under the guise of massaging him, began to search for inconspicuous injuries or disease. Nothing. Moe didn't seem to need fixing in any sense of the word.

Saturday. Laundry day. One week since Jim had died. Maxey collected the dirty wash and slapped it into a plastic basket as if it were to blame.

The phone rang as she hefted the load onto one hip, ready to go out the door, and a frisson of déjà vu skipped down her backbone. She waited while Ernestine did her stuff.

The caller's voice wasn't familiar, and neither was his name. She let him get as far as, "I have this motel in Fort Collins—" and seeing a you-have-won-a-weekend scam coming, she turned and walked out.

She felt foolish, down on her knees checking her car for explosives. But she preferred foolishness to nagging apprehension.

"Lose something?"

Turning her face, she saw two narrow moccasins beside her on the pavement. She eyed the hairy, muscular legs up to a pair of knife-creased white walking shorts, and had to brace herself on the flank of the car to finish the visual trip to Leo Crown's face.

"Morning," he said, flashing his teeth.

"Morning." She stood and dusted her hands. "What can I do for you?"

He leaned against the Toyota, an arm draped gracefully along the roof. "Mr. Macy is rather put out with me because the mills of insurance are grinding exceedingly slow. I wanted to explain to you where the problem lies."

"Go ahead." She crossed her arms and looked attentive.

"I realize that you and he were married once and are friends still, so this is not going to be easy for you to accept." He ran a hand along the nape of his neck. "We have reason to believe that Mr. Macy isn't telling all he knows about Jim Donovan's murder."

"What is it 'we' think he isn't telling?" She would let him have one more minute to pussyfoot, and then she was going to say something crude.

"It's come to our attention," Crown said, leaning into her and lowering his voice while a boy on a bicycle pedaled past, as if the kid were a spy, "that Reece Macy has run up some pretty large debts that he couldn't possibly pay off on his normal salary. As you know, he doesn't have an alibi—"

"The police don't seem too interested in Reece as a murder suspect," she said, making him dance sideways by jerking open the rear door. "And anyway, if you think Reece is going to get rich from running the *Regard,* you're crazy." She hurled the laundry basket into the backseat.

"Oh, *I* don't. It's the corporate office that—"

She slid into the front seat and fearlessly started the motor. *Bang!* The slap on the roof made her heart gallop for several seconds. Glaring at Leo Crown's blandly innocent face, she shoved the gear and let off the brake too fast, laying rubber for the first time since puberty.

The coin laundry was steamy hot, perfect for her mood. Maxey thumped her clothes basket in front of the last two washers together and began slam-dunking towels into one.

Reece might be a liar and a cheat, but he wasn't a killer. She couldn't have married and made love to—not necessarily in that order—a killer.

Besides, Reece knew as well as she did that the *Regard* was going to be a break-even venture, if not forever, at least for now, when he allegedly needed funds.

Besides, Reece and Jim were friends, kindred souls in their interests and outlooks—both of them Democrats, environmentalists, agnostics, sports unenthusiasts, and literature buffs. Reece blast this brotherhood to kingdom come? Never.

Besides—Maxey pressed quarters in the metal slots and pushed/pulled viciously—Reece was too lazy to commit murder.

Slumping into the pink dinette chair farthest from anyone with children, Maxey whipped open a 1979 issue of *Good Housekeeping* someone had left behind and began to read how to make a ten-layered torte, as if she really cared.

Much as he loved machines, Grady hated answering machines. Here he'd finally made up his mind and been all primed to do it, and she wasn't there. So now he could debate with himself some more.

It was too pretty a day to go straight home. Maxey indulged herself by driving up Flagstaff Mountain and sitting on the wall overlooking Boulder long enough to experience several mood changes, including depression, exhilaration, and serious craving for a romantic interlude. Coming home the long, back way through Gold Hill, she saw two deer, three chipmunks, and a raccoon, and the best part about it was they were all alive and well.

By the time she was stomping upstairs with her clean, well-traveled laundry, she felt reasonably cheerful and ready to face another week. Moe yowled at her to hurry.

Having him around was a good excuse for talking to herself. "Coming, coming. We'll eat, and then we'll clean house, and then maybe we'll rent a movie. How about *Cat on a Hot Tin Roof?* Have you seen that one yet? Or *Cat Ballou? Kitty Foyle?*" She interrupted this game to punch her telephone playback.

The first thing on it was Rita. She spun the tape past that.

" . . . motel in Fort Collins—"

"Yeah, yeah, yeah," she muttered, fast-forwarding.

" . . . Crown, here."

She stuck out her tongue but continued to listen.

"You don't need to call me back. Just thought you ought to know that one of Reece's creditors is a gambling casino in Vegas. I just don't want you to get dragged down if he goes. I mean whether or not he did anything lethal. Call me anytime, if you need anything whatso—"

She smacked the fast forward, not sure if she was more angry at Crown or at Reece.

"Ms. Burnell, this is Wes Fawcett calling from Grand Junction about your reward for information about Mr. Donovan's death."

Maxey whipped up a pencil and scratch pad to jot down the phone number and squirmed onto a stool at the counter to return his call.

14

The same voice answered, "Fawcett Storage."

"Mr. Fawcett? Maxey Burnell. Did you have something that might help us solve Jim's murder?" She shut her eyes, the better to hear.

"Maybe. It might not be anything, but you can decide. See, back on April twenty-fourth, this man came in the office wanting to rent a space. Gave his name as Jim Donovan and address as Ten Regard Street in Boulder."

"My gosh, how did you remember that after all this time?"

"Well, see, we go over our records on a regular schedule, check on who hasn't paid their rent, and he hasn't. When I mailed a reminder, it came back stamped 'no such address.' So then I thought the name sounded familiar, and pretty soon I put it together."

"And why did you think Jim's murder was connected with his storing something there?" She smoothed at the frown line between her eyes with the eraser of the pencil.

"Well, see, it's in the contract we can inspect the storage unit if there's nonpayment. People sometimes leave town and take their property without our knowing."

"And?"

"And, well, see, Mr. Donovan's unit was still full of his stuff."

While she listened her mind was trying to imagine why Jim would have gone clear across the state to rent storage space. "What kind of stuff?"

"Guns."

The phone twisted in her convulsive grip. She fumbled it straighter to her ear. "Guns?"

"That's right. Nothing but guns."

"What kind?" she asked, still stupid with surprise.

"All kinds. Handguns and rifles and shotguns."

"An *arsenal*?"

"Oh, no, just maybe—oh—twenty."

Even one was too many for Jim Donovan, staunch enemy of the NRA. What was going on here? What else should she ask to make this come clear?

"What did this Jim Donovan look like?"

"Oh. Golly, I couldn't say. After all this time. Even if you put him in a lineup, I sure do doubt I could find him."

"How did he pay when he paid?" Squeezing the receiver between shoulder and ear, Maxey reached for her purse and began sorting through it. "Personal check? Credit card?"

"The one deposit he made was cash. He picked the quarterly payment plan. And so the rent's not past due very long, but I figure since he's dead—"

"Yes, yes. I'll pay you whatever's owed. I'll drive over sometime the first of this week. Just sit tight and leave it all exactly the way he left it, okay? Don't throw anything out on the sidewalk."

"Oh, golly, I wouldn't—"

She found the photograph and slapped it onto the counter. "What's your address, Mr. Fawcett?"

While he told her she wrote automatically. Rita had said that her husband sold off his guns in Grand Junction about four months ago. Maxey could suddenly empathize with Reece and his alleged gambling. Because right now she'd bet anything—she'd just found Jerald's gun accumulation.

Why? Why would Jim Donovan have bought Jerald Stamp's—or anyone else's—guns?

She thanked Fawcett, disconnected, and tried Sam's home number.

"Yeah, hello."

"Hi there. You sound like your usual happy self."

"Who is this?"

Mortified, she snapped, "Well, it isn't *Max* Burnell."

There might have been an infinitesimal softening

in his voice when he said, "Hi, what can I do for you?"

"I just had a conversation with a man in Grand Junction who runs a storage business. He says our Jim rented a unit last spring and it's full of guns."

He grunted.

"And, Sam, I'm almost positive he got them from Jerald Stamp."

"Who?"

She rolled her eyes and hunched closer to the mouthpiece. "Did I wake you out of a sound sleep? Jerald Stamp. The guy whose wife we—"

"Oh, yeah. What makes you think that?"

She explained with growing impatience for Sam's obvious lack of enthusiasm. "So how about you and me driving over to Grand Junction tomorrow and checking it out?"

"Tomorrow's Sunday."

"So?"

"It's my day off."

"It's my day off, too! What kind of detective are you?"

"Not the kind you read about in books. Not Dirty Harry. I like to have some time of my own away from the job."

"Fine. We'll call it a date. Take a picnic lunch."

"Sorry. I've got other plans. Let's do it Monday."

She wanted to turn *him* down. "Okay. If I don't go without you tomorrow."

"Don't do that!" She'd aroused his interest at last, but before she could congratulate herself on his caring about her, he added, "You'll contaminate the evidence. We need to dust for fingerprints, is the main thing."

Well. It wasn't the first time Maxey had dated a man a couple times and been disappointed. Apparently he hadn't liked being asked personal questions like "What is your phone number?" and "Why aren't you married?" Another stud imagining he was being herded into a rendering plant.

"Catch you later, then," she said.

"Maxey? Give me a rain check, huh? I've got a migraine that's squeezing the hair right out of my head."

"Sure. I'm sorry," she said, and heard him hang up.

She slapped the receiver onto the cradle with an explosive, "Damn!" Chin on fist, she gazed out the far window at clouds gliding east as smoothly as if on conveyer belts. Feeling her eyelids begin to droop from the sky's hypnotic flow, she stood and stretched, her joints cracking. The ringing phone made her groan.

She finished rolling her shoulders before answering. "Hello?"

Silence.

"Hello!" she demanded, thinking of Rita's mysterious telephone calls.

"Oh, I was waiting for the beep. Is this Miss Burnell?"

"Yes."

"Great. Am I glad I caught—I know I left you a

message earlier, but I think he's getting ready to leave. For good."

"Who's getting ready to leave? And who are you?"

"Mr. Donovan's murderer. I mean that's who's checking out. I'm the motel manager."

Maxey sank onto her stool again. "Where are you, did you say? Fort Collins? And how do you know this man killed Jim?"

"I don't know it for sure. So I don't want to call in the police. It's kind of involved. I don't want to try to explain on the phone. Could you come up here?"

She readied pencil over paper once again. "What's the name of the place?"

"The Come On Inn. And my name's Grady. But I got to tell you there are some things I've got to have your promise will be off the record."

"I'll certainly try to work with you on that, Mr. Grady. Give me directions how to find you."

"It's just 'Grady,' and we're on 287, right on the south edge of town."

While she scribbled his more explicit directions she was already calculating the quickest way to get there. It would take at least an hour, hour and a half.

"Grady, are you sure you don't have enough on this guy to bring the cops in?" She checked that she had everything in her shoulder bag, including the photo of Jerald Stamp.

"I know I don't. And there's another reason I

don't want to get involved with the police."

Uh-oh. "You're wanted for something yourself?"

"No, nothing like that. Just come as soon as you can." He didn't wait for her to have the last word.

Maxey sat thinking so hard and long, the forgotten receiver began its authoritarian, "If you'd like to make a call, please hang up and try again."

She ought to call Sam, but his headache and consequent indifference to her sleuthing would undoubtedly result in another rebuff. Or he'd tell her to phone the Fort Collins police. Which she could do once she reached the Come On Inn, after she'd found out exactly what Grady had to offer.

Throwing a handful of dry cat food into Moe's bowl, she considered taking Reece along. But when she dialed, there was no response, not even from an answering machine.

Never mind. Anything he could do, she could do better, anyway.

She locked the apartment, ran downstairs, peered under her car, and started it up for the trip to Fort Collins.

The Come On Inn was easy enough to find, but it wasn't the kind of place Maxie would ordinarily have been looking for. Of fifties vintage, the shellacked yellow log exterior and skinny black wrought-iron roof supports forecasted interiors with chenille bedspreads, echoing shower stalls, and the cloying scent of germicide. There were four vehicles parked like horses at hitching posts, two from out of state and two with Colorado plates.

Maxey crunched across the gravel apron toward her reflection in the picture window of the office. A baby dust devil capered across her path, stinging her ankles, bare between jeans and sandals. The sky had the gray luminescence of dusk complicated by storm clouds. Turning the doorknob, she stepped out of the noise of whining traffic into the relative quiet of a typical mom-and-pop motel office, TV audible in the distance.

The man who immediately came through a rear doorway was smiling shy welcome. "Help you?"

"Grady? I'm Maxey Burnell."

He gave this some consideration. "You're better looking than your picture in the paper."

"Thank God for that. So is your murder suspect still here?" She put her shoulder bag on the floor and folded her arms on Grady's counter.

"Yes."

"Well?"

He had a rubber band that he stretched and relaxed, over and over, while he contemplated where to begin his story. Maxey wanted to swat it out of his hand. She showed her own nonchalance by crossing her knees and clumsily stepping on her bag.

Reaching down to retrieve Jerald's photograph from it, she said, "First off, does your guest look like this?"

He lifted the picture into the light. "This's Jerald Stamp."

Maxey blinked. "You know Jerald Stamp? Is he here?"

"No, no. I just know him from his picture in the papers and on TV. The guy in twelve isn't Jerald Stamp. He's too old."

"What's your man's name?" She put the photo back in her bag, definitely disappointed.

"Ken Oakley." The rubber band broke at last, and Grady picked up a pen to jiggle. "His wife did the checking in, and her name's Anita."

"Which car is his?" She backed carefully to the door and peered up the line.

"The white Taurus. It's a rental. He's been loading stuff in the trunk, so I think he's about to vacate the room. I was expecting it because he had this big blowup with his wife and there wouldn't be much reason I know of for him to hang around anymore."

Maxey returned to the counter and leaned conspiratorially over it. "So why do you think he's Jim's murderer?"

"I heard him on the phone with his wife last night. Really it was more like one o'clock this morning. What he said was, 'It's nothing to get shot in the head. One little hole, big deal. Now, Jim Donovan, that's a different matter. When he went, he *went*. A hell of a way to die. Bet you didn't know I know something about explosives. You want to worry about that a little whenever you start your car from now—'"

"Wait a minute!" Maxey waved her hands to stop the recital. "How can you remember all that? You can't really remember all that."

"It might not be exact, but it's close. I'm a real good listener." Grady gave her the very same injured look that Reece used to give her the nights he came home after midnight, full of excuses.

"And how'd you happen to overhear this conversation?"

He had the decency to blush. "Oakley had been acting kind of strange, so I listened in when he phoned the missus. In case he was going to hold up the motel or something." He dropped the pen and didn't attempt to recover it. "I was on the switchboard."

Maxey continued to subject him to an unsmiling examination.

"Yup," he said, folding his arms and rocking on his heels. "Just listened on the switchboard."

"And what was that business at the first, about a shooting death being easy?" It was probably a waste of time discussing one flake with another flake, but what the heck. She didn't have any movies rented for tonight.

"Uh-huh, that's another thing. It's a real coincidence, you having that photo with you. Oakley and his wife were discussing Rita Stamp's suicide."

"I suppose you remember that word for word, too?"

"Sure," he said promptly. "Oakley goes, 'You heard about Mrs. Stamp, didn't you?' And Anita goes, 'God, yes. Stupid, stupid woman. Thinking she couldn't live without one particular man when there's so many men in the world.'"

Grady's voice had gone falsetto on Mrs. Oakley's part of the dialogue, which somehow gave credibility to it. Maxey found herself holding her breath.

"So then Oakley says, 'What you driving at, honey?' and I tell you, if he said it to me like that—without the 'honey,' of course—I wouldn't have answered back as sharp as his wife did. I mean it was spooky. Full of threat, you know?"

Maxey nodded, spellbound. "What did she answer back?"

"'I'm driving at us being through. You're too much for me. I don't want any part of your life from here on out.' And he goes, 'What's the matter, babe? A little suicide got your conscience riled up?' And then's when he said that about the bullet being nothing and Donovan's death being something."

"Uh-huh. How'd that go again?"

Grady repeated it, word for word the same, if her own faulty memory was any judge.

"I want to get a look at this Oakley. Is he in his room now?"

Grady shook his head. "He's walked up the road to have supper."

If she were Nancy Drew, she'd use the opportunity to snoop in his room. In reality, the idea didn't tempt her in the slightest.

She paced the little room in time with her

thoughts. "All you've given me so far is hearsay. I don't think the police would be interested, and I know a judge wouldn't. Even if Oakley said what you say he said, he could have been just bragging, trying to scare his wife. Though it does sound like they knew Rita Stamp."

"Here he comes now."

Maxey stopped on a dime and swiveled to peer out the window. A male figure was crossing the parking lot from the highway, head down, arms swinging, his gait suggestive of a limp.

"What's he carrying?" Maxey felt the irrational inclination to whisper.

"Probably a doggie bag."

"Doggie bag?"

"Yeah, that's another thing. It's against motel rules, but it's only been for a couple of days and I have to admit Oakley's got me too nervous to—"

"Doggie bag!" If Grady had been wearing lapels, Maxey would have been clutching them.

15

"*Oh, gosh, he's coming* in here," Grady said. He scuffled his feet as if he couldn't decide which way to run.

"Sign me in," Maxey said, leaning over the counter.

"Huh?"

"Sign me in. Pretend I'm here to spend the night. Give me a room."

The door gusted open behind her, and she resisted the urge to whirl around.

Grady fumbled a registration card down in front of her and bent to get a key. "Just the one night, then?" he ad-libbed.

"Right." She signed her mother's maiden name and made up a license-plate number before turning with casual deliberateness to smile at the old man by the door.

He stood with one hand resting on his hip, the other dangling a greasy brown bag that had dribbled a thread of stain on one floppy pants leg. Complexion like warm putty. Hair and whiskers in need of a trim. Eyes as clear and knowing as a lion on the stalk.

She exchanged a nod with him and returned her attention to Grady.

"Fourteen. Straight up the line. You can't miss it, except it comes right after twelve. There's no thirteen because people are superstitious," he babbled, and then, "Oh, no!" he said, with an expression of such horror, Maxey was sure Oakley must have produced an assault rifle. "Winnie! What's she doing here?"

Turning, Maxey saw a silver Cadillac sliding to a stop under the portico. A wiry woman with a butch haircut got out.

Maxey grabbed up the room key and prepared to escape past Oakley, who was bumped forward as the Caddy driver charged through the door. The three of them danced momentarily, till the newcomer broke free and pushed through the counter's swinging gate.

"I'll be checking out in the morning," Oakley called, still blocking Maxey's exit.

She turned around with one last message of her own. "Mr. uhhh—" Grady's last name had slipped through Maxey's memory. "You remember that phone call I wanted to make? Would you put that through right away, please?" Maxey gave him as meaningful a look as she dared.

"Mm-hmm," Grady said, obviously distracted by the woman who was now pawing through papers on the far desk.

Oakley pushed the door open and motioned Maxey past his outstretched arm. Careful not to touch him, she went out. He smelled of beer and cooking grease.

Conscious of Oakley's footsteps behind her as she walked the row of rooms, Maxey jingled her key with forced nonchalance. His shoes stopped at twelve, and she veered onto the doormat of fourteen, certain he was watching her.

She was never good with unfamiliar locks, especially when she was in a hurry and on the nervous side. The key slid in and wouldn't turn. To make the nightmare worse, in Oakley's room a dog began to bark.

"Help you?" Oakley moved fast for his age. His freckled fingers took the key away and wound it with a deft twist. The door fell open.

"Thanks. You make it look easy." Maxey held out her hand for the key. She remembered feeling like this when she was eight years old, striking her first match.

Oakley tapped her key against his chin, studying her. "Say. Aren't you Maxey Burnell?"

"I'm afraid you—"

"Sure you are. I read you all the time." His old-man voice quavered with enthusiasm.

It was highly unlikely he'd recognized her

from her column photograph. Across his shoulder she could see her little Toyota, its vanity plate proclaiming *Maxey*.

"That's okay," he assured her with a wink. "You're here on the quiet, right? Meeting someone, right?" The teasing words didn't match the watchfulness in his eyes.

"Something like that," she agreed, wiggling her fingers to remind him she needed her key.

"How about an autograph?" he said, and snaking an arm around her back, he lockstepped her into the room and kicked the door shut.

Spinning out of his grasp, she reached for the doorknob and winced as his palm clamped her fingers to the cool metal.

Trying not to inhale his malty breath, trying to mirror the coldness in the flat eyes inches from hers, Maxey said, "Get the hell out of my room."

His lips twitched against amusement. "Why don't you sit down, Ms. Burnell, and tell me why you're really here."

Now her stomach swooped like the time she'd dropped the match and set loose an avid flame. She'd had the wit to extinguish that danger. This time—

He let go of her hand to grip her forearm and lead her to the bed. She'd been wrong about the chenille spread. This one was a faded, woven paisley—

"Hey! Answer me!" he demanded, pushing her down on it.

She folded her arms and narrowed her eyes at him, jaw set. The dog next door hiccuped three last barks, and then the prevalent sound was the air-conditioning unit. Maxey's limbs vibrated in time with it.

Oakley put his hands on his knees and leaned at her. "Maxey?" His voice wasn't old anymore.

She tried to think what to do or say. Instead she was thinking dumb thoughts like *where is the doggie bag?*

No one had ever slapped her face before. Her first reaction was surprise, followed closely by humiliation, outrage, and the devout hope that no one would ever do it again. Touching her stinging cheek with palsied fingers, she blinked against tears before raising her eyes to glare at him again.

"What is your problem, Oakley?"

"Oh, it isn't me that has a problem."

She'd seen plenty of movie villains smile like this, like they were enjoying their work.

Oh, Grady, please, please be phoning the police.

Grady was watching his mother shuffle through his mail.

"What are you looking for, Winnie?" he repeated.

"Some kind of proof that you're working on the permit to turn this place into an office complex." She hesitated over a renewal notice from *Popular Mechanix*, tossed it at the wastebasket, and kept sorting.

"It's all been on the phone," he fibbed. "Nothing in writing yet. There's a board got to meet the end of this month to okay it."

"Good. I'm bringing a client to look at the building next weekend. Have Josie wash these windows. What's your apartment look like?" and she marched in that direction.

"I'll straighten up better on Friday!"

He rushed ahead of her to slam the bedroom door and stand guard. He'd gotten careless about his surveillance equipment, because she'd never made an inspection tour before.

"What's wrong with that room?" she was quick to demand.

"It's like a tornado hit. I'm building a model. I'll be done and cleaned up in a week. Promise."

Her nostrils flared once as if she smelled something fishy, but then she went to punch off the television set, saying, "I could use a cold drink."

"Sure, Winnie. Sprite? A beer?" He followed her into the kitchenette, hoping she didn't plan to stay the night.

"Show you a trick?" Oakley suggested slyly, sitting down beside Maxey on the bed and squeezing her knee so she couldn't slide away. "Watch this."

He pinched the flesh of his sagging jowl and pulled. A glob of skin and tissue came loose, leaving a ragged spot like a hole in a sock.

"'Mission Impossible.' 'Twilight Zone.'" He rolled his forefinger down his cheek and left a furrowed scar.

Maxey knew he was trying to terrify her. She wanted her damnedest not to gratify him. But the sight of this middle-aged man emerging from the shell of an old man was pretty unnerving.

Well, hell, what she ought to do was scream her head off. She opened her mouth.

"Don't," he said, yanking up one of his pants legs. Next moment he was showing her the undesirable end of the little pistol he'd had holstered to that pale, hairy calf.

"Opera." She congratulated herself on getting that one word out above a whisper and below a scream.

"Yes?"

"Rita said her husband loved opera. I thought she meant as a spectator. You dress up and make up and sing."

"You're two thirds right. I carry spears or torches or whatever the extras are needed to do. Help with costumes. And makeup. I can't really clean this off properly without a washrag and spirit-gum remover, but you get the picture." He flicked the putty from his fingers to the carpet.

A truck downshifted on the highway. *There's a man out there on his way to a hot meal and a bath, perfectly oblivious to me in here talking to death.*

"But enough about me," Jerald Stamp said. "I

want to know about you and how you tracked me here."

"I didn't," she insisted. "It's a coincidence. My boyfriend will be here any minute, expecting me to have the lights low and the bed turned down. He's a Boulder policeman."

He started back in mock fear. "Must be the chief or something if you have to come all the way up here to do your sneaking around. A wife and a dozen kids, no doubt." He watched her. Said softly, "Dim lights and the bed turned down, huh?"

She had seen Moe toy with a cricket before eating it. If she lived, she would never let him do that again.

But she also wasn't going to play the passive cricket. Straightening her shoulders, she said, "Why did you hide from Rita?"

"Because she was a silly cunt." He began to crack his knuckles methodically, the gun held negligently in his hand. "Always hanging on me. Never having an original thought of her own. When our personal finances began to ooze downhill, her only contribution was blind faith that good old Jerald could turn it around."

"You should have been proud that she—"

"I wasn't proud of anything about that woman. She was pretty when I married her, and that lasted about two years, and from then on she was an anchor around my neck."

"You could have divorced—"

"She wasn't all of it. I'm broke. Creditors hounding me, driving me deeper into the swamp. Tell the truth, Maxey. Hasn't there been just once in your life your troubles seemed so overwhelming, you just wanted to disappear?"

Like about now! She shrugged to demonstrate . she was listening.

"So there I am, desperate. And hanging on to a sales-rep territory by my toenails. And driving through Colorado Springs, I stop for a beer. And there's this gorgeous blond lady giving me the eye from halfway down the bar."

Oakley relaxed back on his elbows on the bed, absorbed in his remembrances. Maxey gauged the distance to the door, saw the chain was in place. When the devil did he have time to put that on? she thought. Isn't it about time to hear some sirens?

"Anita Oakley was like a drink from the fountain of youth. She gave me hope. The idea of my disappearing was a kick. She loved it, the planning of it. And where she worked, the job she had was perfect. Want to guess?"

For a moment Maxey was lost, not even sure of the question. Then her subconscious rescued her with, "Highway department. Anita was a flagman or something."

"You're right the first time. When I got out of my car at the roadblock, she was waiting back down the line with a pickup truck and an extra hard hat. We tooled out of there, me with my arm out the window, a union man taking a coffee break. Nobody gave us a second glance. Not even a first glance."

"And you hid out at her place."

"Right again. A couple days. Then she drove me over here. She was going to quit her job— get fired, if possible, so no one would wonder about her leaving right after my disappearance. But now . . ."

Stamp's voice trailed off into silence that, as it lengthened, made Maxey hope he was contemplating his sins. Stealing a glance at him, she could see that whatever he was contemplating, it wasn't making him remorseful. While his mouth drew tighter and his eyes went from chilly to freezing, she sat still and small, trying to blend in with the surroundings.

The air conditioner rattled. Traffic rumbled. No sirens warbled.

"Anita was very good in bed," Stamp said with low, suggestive inflection. "Creative. Insatiable. Willing. The opposite in every way from my lawful wedded wife. Nita brought out appetites in me I had no idea in the world I possessed. Made me grieve for what I'd been missing."

Rolling toward her, Stamp rested his hand on Maxey's forearm. She couldn't help looking up, getting snarled in those predatory eyes.

He said, "Anyone know you're here?"

"I told you. My boyfriend—"

The slap, this time, dropped her on her back,

and before she could scramble up, he had her pinned to the mattress by her throat.

"I think I can safely assume," he whispered in her face, "that I have all the time in the world to do to you whatever I want."

There wasn't much point in pretending she didn't know what he was talking about. Maxey could feel her courage eroding as inexorably as Stamp's finances.

When his hold eased, she licked her smarting lips. "Why did you kill Rita?"

The restraining hand loosened enough to begin a slow, horrible massage of her neck and jaw and cheek. "For all the same reasons I left her in the first place. But mostly because she caught me in the house that night, and I knew she'd never keep it a secret. It's her own fault. I kept phoning home, trying to find a time when she was out, but the stupid bitch never *went* anywhere."

"What did you need from the house?"

"My dog." He laughed. "I was lonesome and feeling sorry for myself, I really missed good old Alf."

"How'd you get Rita to phone me and say what she said?"

He snorted and casually scratched his ear with the butt of the gun. "She thought I was taking her away with me to be some kind of underground moll or something. She wanted to let you know so you wouldn't worry—wasn't that thoughtful of her? So I says, 'Give your friend Maxey a call and tell her you can't take it anymore.' Her next line was supposed to be, 'Don't try to find me,' but of course I didn't give her the chance to get to that."

"Uhhh!" Maxey couldn't help crying as his hand glided down into her cleavage. "Please don't do that."

"Shhh." He gently tapped the gun against her shoulder. "If I was a scientist," he crooned, "you know what I'd research? I'd check out the correlation between fear and sexual desire. Huh? Good idea, huh?"

Squeezing her eyes shut, Maxey remembered telling Grady the police wouldn't be interested in his hearsay evidence against Oakley. And then before she could explain to him the significance of the doggie bag, Oakley had come in. Grady didn't know she was trapped in this room with Jerald Stamp.

The rush of despair felt like a fall from a very great height.

Stamp made a purposeful move toward the waistband of her jeans, and she stammered, "What about Jim Donovan?"

"What *about* Jim Donovan?"

"Why did you kill him?"

"I didn't."

"You must have. You used his name to store your guns in Grand Junction."

"You found out about that, too?" First he frowned and then he laughed as if she were delightfully amusing. "The world's going to lose a regular Sherlock here."

"And you're going to lose your precious guns for past-due rent," she said, hoping to keep him side-tracked.

"Thanks for the warning. I'll put a money order in the mail." Giving his head a deprecating shake, he added, "Even when my bank account was running on empty, I just couldn't bring myself to part with those guns. I told Rita I'd sold them, but really they just disappeared. Like me."

"Why'd you use Jim's name?"

"Spite." His chuckle was deceptively pleasant. "I'd been putting want ads in the local papers like I was really trying to sell off my collection. So I was in the *Regard* office. You weren't there."

I sure wasn't, she thought. And not even aware of my great good fortune.

"So old Donovan got on his high horse about gun control, said he wouldn't run my ad. I called him some appropriate names and he tried to throw me out the door." Stamp sat recalling it and muttered some of the appropriate names.

She felt the weight of air inflating, deflating her lungs.

Brightening, he turned to her again. "So I was still mad when I got to the Junction, and I needed a false name, so I gave his. Sort of poetic justice, you see."

"And you sent him a couple poison-pen letters. Threatened him on the phone."

Shaking his head, looking baffled, he convinced her.

"Okay," she said. "Okay. But then why did you go and blow up his car?"

"I didn't."

"You did!"

They were beginning to sound like argumentative schoolmates.

He recognized the incongruity of it, too. Bending toward her, he bestowed another crocodile smile.

"Honey, I'm about to rape you. And then I'm going to murder you some way or another. But, sweetheart, I would never *lie* to you."

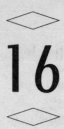

16

"*What do you mean,* 'Am I sure?' You'd have to be deaf not to hear it. There's a dog in one of our rooms. Twelve, sounded like."

Grady scurried behind Winnie on the sidewalk, not eager to confront Oakley himself, but curious to observe what effect his mother would have on old evil eye.

She continued to grumble, "People have some nerve. It says right on the door, rules and regulations. No pets."

Winnie stomped up to number twelve, listened a moment, and rapped smartly. Barking erupted inside, making her throw a triumphant smirk at Grady. She stepped back, hands on hips, to wait.

"Guess he's not home," Grady said, half-relieved and half-disappointed.

"Isn't that his car?" Winnie nodded at the Taurus parked in twelve's space, big as you please.

"He's probably walked up the road to the tavern or somewhere."

The dog's vocalizations were now accompanied by nails scratching wood.

"Just listen to what the dang thing's doing to our property," Winnie exclaimed, and she whirled around to scuttle toward the office.

"Now what are you doing?" Grady asked, catching up as she snatched the master key ring from its desk drawer.

"The dog's owner is probably hiding in there, afraid we're going to evict him. And, by damn, he's right."

"No, Mom! You can't go in there. That animal sounds like he could take your head off!"

"Oh. Yeah." She was actually paying attention to him for once. "Well, then, I'm just going to sit out front here and watch for the owner to come out or come back or whatever."

"Why don't you let me handle it? No use you hanging around for an unpleasant job that I can do myself."

"You won't, though. You'll let it slide."

"No, honest. I'll make him leave. Cross my heart."

"Well, I did want to run over to Aunt Paula's before I drive back to the lake."

"Sure. It'd be a shame to let this little incident ruin your evening."

"What time is it? Oh, lordy, turn on the television. I'm about to miss the lottery drawing."

Jerald Stamp hauled out her shirttail and ripped off the bottom for a gag. "So you won't forget and get too loud," he said, attempting to tie it, the pistol still in one hand.

"No, wait," she struggled to say before it was too late. "I have something to tell you."

"Oh, you do, do you?" Sinking back on his haunches, he made a show of checking his wristwatch. "You got exactly three minutes."

Actually there was nothing to say. What could she possibly have to tell him? *I don't want to suffer and die? Damn you to eternal hellfire? You'll be sorry, because I've got herpes?*

No, definitely not that last, because then he'd surely skip the fate worse than death and go straight to the death part. At the moment her single-minded goal was to keep on breathing.

How could she concentrate with him staring at her and his mangy dog yapping like a maniac next door?

Stamp consulted his watch, and she blurted, "I left a note, outlining my suspicions about you. For my friend the cop."

"You didn't even know who I was till about fifteen minutes ago," Stamp said. "Care to make up a better story?"

"I'll give you money. You need money, right?

Everything I have in the bank. You can tie me up in my apartment or something and disappear again. Believe me, I'd never hunt for you. I never want to even hear your name again."

"Now, that's a little better." Thoughtful, he rubbed at his chin, and a ribbon of artificial flesh peeled away from it. "How much money have you got?"

"Ten, twenty thousand," she fabricated, and saw his disappointment. "Fifty! It's fifty or sixty, I'm sure."

"Come on, Maxey. A smart lady like you ought to do better than this. I know and you know, all you're doing is stringing me. If you can't do it with a little more imagination, I'll have to call off your grace period on account of boredom."

He was right. She was smart, probably smarter than Stamp. And, by God, he wasn't going to use her and leave her body somewhere like so much garbage and get away with it.

"I have to go to the bathroom."

He sighed, running low on patience. "You can use the bathroom, but you can't shut the door. Because I'll be standing in it."

"Big, strong, superior man." She sneered. "Scared of a woman unless he's standing watch with a gun."

"That's right," he said, not falling for that ploy either.

Scooting to the edge of the mattress, she stood up, keeping him in her peripheral vision, ready to

take advantage of any escape opportunity he'd
give her. He stood up, too, an arm's length behind
as she tried to walk instead of stumble toward the
bathroom.

The bleak little porcelain-and-tile room was
pretty much the way she'd pictured it, right down
to the echoing shower stall. She stopped in front of
the yellow-bowled sink and eyed Stamp's reflection
in the dim mirror.

"Come on, Jerald. I can't do my job with you
staring at me. Look at this. What could I possibly
find in here to help me get away from you? There
isn't even a window."

"Maybe it turns me on to watch women pee."
He had to laugh alone.

"I won't waste my time screaming," she said. "If
anyone heard me over your crummy dog, they'd
think it was the television. You'd be in here so fast,
I wouldn't have a chance to really crank it up full
volume. Let me have a few minutes' privacy here."

His mouth twitched in that annoying, superior-
and-proud-of-it suggestion of a grin. "Okay,
Maxey. You can have another three minutes.
But no locking the door. Anything seems suspicious, I'm coming in."

Habit made her start to thank him. She closed
the door gently, felt the latch engage with a quiet
click, and it was all she could do to keep from turning the seductive lock.

She sat down on the toilet, fully clothed, and
scanned the room for something to use against

Stamp. That was no lie about there being nothing here to help her. Sink. Soap. Plastic glasses in plastic wrap. One washcloth, one hand towel, one bath towel, one bath mat—all white—lined up on one chrome towel bar. Plastic hook on the back of the door. One round wastebasket the size and weight of a child's sand bucket.

"Having any luck, sweetheart?" Stamp's voice was surprisingly loud through the door.

No, she thought, and not the kind you mean either. Maxey reached over to turn on the sink tap slightly, for the sound effect. Careful not to make any other noise, she stood up, turned around, and lifted the lid off the toilet tank. No bricks. Nothing lethal looking except the slimy water, which she doubted she could get Stamp to drink.

Replacing the lid as quietly as she'd hefted it, she stretched to draw back the shower curtain. Three empty walls, one empty floor.

"Time's about up," Stamp said.

She leaped to shut off the water and flushed the toilet. "Give me another minute. I don't feel so good."

That seemed to strike him as hilarious. She didn't have time to appreciate why. The only thing in here that has any potential at all is the threadbare towels. If I could whip one around his gun hand or his throat . . . Or what am I wearing that might work better for that?

The commode stopped running and she flushed

it again. Jerking her shirt off over her head, she reached behind and undid the white bra. Wrestled the shirt back on. Stared at the configuration of lace and elastic, straps and cups.

A sling, she thought desperately. A cosh. Put something heavy in it and bash him first chance I get.

What, though? Everything was too light or nailed down.

"Maa-xee."

She rolled her eyes upward, about to concede, and focused on the shower spigot. And almost shouted, *Eureka!*

"I'm always this close," Winnie said, turning away from the TV. "They just rig it so I'll keep buying tickets. Teasing me. I've got a good mind not to play the lottery anymore. Show them I'm above that kind of monkey business."

She picked up her white plastic purse and seemed to be exiting. Grady tried not to look too eager about that.

They walked as far as the office before Winnie gave him a pop quiz. "What is it you have to do yet this evening?"

For a bad moment his mind spun wheels uselessly. Then his darting eyes collided with the pale outline of Oakley's Taurus.

"Get rid of the dog."

"I might stop back later to be sure."

"For gosh sake, Mom. Oakley's an old geezer. He won't give me any trouble."

The door swung inward, and Stamp stood in it, his expression a cross between suspicion and a leer. Seeing Maxey, fully clothed, standing innocently by the sink, he backed into the main room, motioning with the pistol for her to follow. Obediently she moved forward, inwardly gloating as his guard relaxed and the gun wavered away from her chest toward the wall at her left.

There had been a scary moment when she'd thought the shower head was too corroded to budge, when Stamp's impatience seemed to ooze under the door and weaken her frantic hand. Then the screw threads gave way with a squeak she thought surely he could hear. Five more seconds and she had the spotty, bullet-shaped chrome securely knotted into the bra. And two seconds after that, Stamp pushed the door wide.

Now he said, "You don't look sick to me. Just a little apprehensive. Which, believe me, is justified."

He began to turn to skirt the bed, glanced back at it to check the distance, and she rushed him.

Swinging her found weapon from behind to in front of herself in an overhead arc, she even managed a Miss Piggy "hi-yah!" as she struck down at his wrist.

She had always been a disgustingly poor shot with a flyswatter, probably because she was too squeamish to have a true killer's instinct. But this target was different; she knew the first blow had to do damage or all hope was lost. The spot she'd chosen to aim for was the wrist of Stamp's gun hand.

Like the uncooperative flies, Stamp saw it coming; he lurched backward and half fell across the bed. The shower-head-weighted brassiere smacked into the barrel of the pistol and sent it spinning across the bedspread.

"Uhhh!" Maxey cried out from fear and exertion, fighting to bring the unstable club back into position for another swing.

If Stamp had lunged for the gun, she'd have had him, have hammered the base of his skull. But he was too clever to make that instinctive move. Instead he hurtled forward, tackling Maxey, pinning her hand and its weapon between their bodies as they toppled to the carpet.

Grady sat down at the electronic console in his bedroom and twiddled dials, listening in on room twelve. Pacing paws, a gentle whimper, one sharp yip that hurt Grady's ears—all indicated that the dog was in residence. But where was Oakley? Surely not there, or his mutt wouldn't be so agitated. Unless the old man was there and hurt. Maybe he'd had a heart attack or something.

Pulling at his earlobe, Grady considered whether to try phoning the room. Oakley wouldn't answer, most likely, and then Grady still wouldn't know whether he was away or disabled and in need of help.

Still trying to decide, and more out of habit than with any clear plan, Grady switched on the receiver for the next room, fourteen.

The transmitter in this room was an old, cheap, self-powered bug attached to the frame over the bed that contained a reproduction of Van Gogh's *Sunflowers*. The batteries had to be changed every four or five days and needed it now. Grady frowned as he tried to make sense of the noises filtering through.

Bumps and rustlings and what might have been a groan. If he didn't know better, Grady would have said Miss Burnell was engaging in the kind of activity most of his guests came to engage in.

First Stamp took the bra away from her, prizing it out of her fingers and examining it while he kept her down with a forearm across her neck. When he hurled it toward the bathroom, it rang against the sink and crashed against the tile floor. As he glared down at her and called her names, his spittle peppered her face.

Grady stared at the receiver, horrified. Despite the bad batteries he recognized Oakley's voice. The unpleasant words weren't unusual—Grady had heard similar threatening promises before, between consenting adults who were obviously enjoying it. But none had uttered them with such cold, hair-raising menace. Miss Burnell said something unintelligible that was quick and small and pleading.

Chewing a hangnail, Grady agonized over this new problem. Call the police? Suddenly he remembered Miss Burnell's telling him to make "that phone call." It hadn't registered before, when Winnie was subjecting him to the usual hazing.

Turning down the transmission, Grady picked up the telephone and dialed 9—1—

The shriek, even through the lowered receiver, curled Grady's toes. Oakley was killing that woman. No way would the police ever make it in time.

Slamming the handset onto the cradle, he knocked over his chair getting up and rushed to his closet and tool chest. The crowbar that had come in so handy for saving Josie-in-distress now looked woefully light and inadequate. With less haste Grady walked to the phone again and wavered, irresolute.

Well, what would *Winnie* do?

17

Having rolled her over on the bristly carpet, Stamp was mashing her face into it. His knee came down, sharp in the small of her back.

Something snapped in her nose and warmth gushed toward her upper lip. Teeth aching, tongue dry and gritty, she gasped for air and got only bodily fluids. The sensation of suffocating, of drowning, made her flail her arms uselessly.

Just as fireworks were bursting inside her eyelids his hand loosened, and she sucked a breath so greedy it choked her. Before she could stop coughing, he clutched a fistful of hair and yanked. Now she was a taut bow, neck straining toward spine, his knee still holding her down. She reached with both hands to claw at his, and he rewarded her with a quick shake that sent agony shooting the length of her backbone and down both legs to the tips of both big toes.

He was going to break her. Literally.

At first the noise was only a continuation of the drumming inside her skull, the throbbing of her heart. But then Stamp relaxed his grip and slid his hand around to cover her mouth, and she recognized the sound. Someone was knocking on the door.

Stamp was breathing as hard as she was. He let her head drop, ear to the floor and—blessed relief!—withdrew his knee from the hollow it had surely drilled into her back. Now he was lifting her, hauling her with him to the bed, sitting down on it with her sprawled across his lap, stretching to pick up the pistol where it had fallen.

The knocking had stopped. Maxey strained to hear something hopeful. Like: "Come out with your hands up—you're surrounded."

Instead Grady's reedy voice asked, "Miss Burnell?"

Stamp's hand tightened against her teeth. He obviously wasn't interested in letting her answer.

"Miss Burnell, I've got the extra towels you wanted. And some ice."

Maxey could see a rivulet of bright red oozing below her nose, across Stamp's white knuckles. Her back burned with a dull, monotonous ache.

A key scrabbled at the lock and Stamp jerked to attention. "Hey! Don't come in here," he shouted.

"Sorry," came the answer. "I thought no one was

in. I just want to give these things to Miss Burnell."

Cursing under his breath, Stamp heaved Maxey into the middle of the bed and stood up. "Okay, just a minute, fella. You caught us at a bad time—you know what I mean?"

"Sorry," Grady said again. "It'll only take a minute to hand you this stuff, and I won't bother you anymore."

Stamp's frown swooped to within inches of Maxey's raw face. "You say one word, I shoot him in the stomach. Hear me?"

While she was still struggling to nod he whipped the bedspread over her up to her chin and used a corner of it to scrub clean her tender nose. Holding the pistol straight-armed beside his right leg, the barrel pointed toward the floor, he walked to take off the chain lock.

It had gone dark outside, Maxey saw as the door angled open far enough for Grady to hand through whatever he'd brought. The yellow lamplight behind him fluttered with suicidal moths.

She knew Grady was checking up on her, and she yearned to give him a sign, something he could carry back to the outside world that would give her hope of rescue. But even focusing her eyes on him was difficult. Her usually quick mind, dulled by Stamp's brutalities, had retreated deep inside somewhere, leaving her body to suffer indignities and abuse on its own from now on.

It did occur to her that Stamp didn't know Grady could implicate him in two murders. Soon to be three murders. She could even work her lips into a smile, thinking how Stamp wasn't going to get away with this.

Her eyes drifted toward the door again, where Stamp, standing sideways to conceal the gun, reached out to accept the towels draped on Grady's arm. She could see that Grady was puzzled by this familiar figure in baggy clothes, with Oakley's voice, but with the blurred features of another man's face.

Don't let him see you examining him! she silently warned Grady. And opened her mouth to yell as Stamp's right hand with its deadly appendage began to lift and turn toward the door.

There was no explosion, just a crackle, a hiss. Stamp came flying backward into the room and fell short of the bed, his head clanging the metal frame. For a moment he lay as dead, and then he was twitching, jiggling, dancing on his back.

Maxey was on her knees on the mattress now, hyperventilating through her mouth, eyes fixed on her tormentor laid so mysteriously low. He was trying to talk now, "Uh, uh, uh, uh." A lazy wisp of smoke escaped a scorched spot on his left sleeve.

"Jeez," Grady said, stepping over the dropped towels to venture into the room. "Jeez." He gingerly picked up Stamp's gun and laid it on top of the TV.

"What did you do to him?" Maxey whispered, turning her gaze to the sticklike object in Grady's trembling hand.

"I'm sorry it took so long for me to get here," he said, noticing, with obvious fascination, the condition of her face. "First there was Winnie to get rid of, and then I hadn't used this since I made it about four years ago, so I had to hunt up new batteries. And then I'm on my way out the office door, and this couple drives up wanting a room, and to save time I told them we didn't have a vacancy. Winnie would kill me."

"What did you do to him?"

Grady held up the thing in his hand and examined it as if he'd never seen it before himself. "It's a stun wand. Seventy-five thousand volts. I never used it on anything but a tree before. Jeez."

Jerald Stamp curled into a fetal ball and continued to whimper.

"Oh, God, Grady. Am I glad to see you."

He drew himself straighter and looked pleased.

"But how did you know?" she marveled. "That this guy is dangerous? That you needed that stunamajig and that you had to hit him with it right away?"

"We better get you to a doctor," Grady said, by way of not answering.

"We have to give this snake to the police first. Are they coming?"

He slumped, no longer the conquering hero. "Not exactly."

"What—they're either coming or they aren't!"

"Miss Burnell, do you think you could manage to look at something in my apartment before we call the police? I'll tie Mr. Oakley here first."

"Stamp," she corrected. "That's Jerald Stamp."

"Jeez," he said, leaning for a closer look. "Jeez."

"Look, Grady, I'm hurting. Let's get this over with, okay?"

"Oh, sure." He didn't hesitate about cutting the drapery cord with his pocketknife to hog-tie an unresisting Stamp.

Maxey, shivering with shock, kept the bedspread for the walk to the office, hugging it around herself Indian style. She made a wide detour around room twelve, where Alf's barking had taken on a new frenzy, as if he knew his master was in trouble. Though Maxey hadn't heard rain falling, the concrete was glossy damp, and she could taste the granite tang that her wounded nose couldn't smell.

Following Grady through the office and into his living quarters, Maxey thought that the place could use more windows and less assorted furniture. They ended up in what was obviously his bedroom.

"I've never showed this to anyone before. But . . . This is what I'm worried about," Grady said, waving his arms at what looked like an expensive home-entertainment center. "If you're grateful for my maybe saving your life, would you help me come up with a story for the police so they don't discover this?"

"What is it?" she asked, sidestepping an immediate committal.

The glowing lights reflected in his proud eyes. "I built everything myself. Here, I'll show you." He sat down on a cracked plastic secretarial chair and deftly threw switches. "This is room twelve."

From what looked like an ordinary radio, the sound of Alf's hoarse woofing jumped out at them. For a disconcerting moment, when the dog drew a moist, snuffling breath, Maxey believed that he had somehow found his way from that room to this and was about to jump her.

"Great fidelity, huh?" Grady said. "Now, see, we can check up on Oak—Jerald Stamp by doing this and this."

The result was less impressive. Maxey heard a hum that might have been an air conditioner. Nothing else.

"You have the rooms bugged?" She was torn between being revolted and wanting to praise the Lord. "You heard us talking? Fighting? You listen in to people all the time?"

"Yeah, but it's not like you think," Grady pleaded. "It isn't the private stuff, the *people,* that I'm interested in. I'm no pervert. I just like the electronics. The gimmicks. Building something complicated just for the challenge and fun of having it work."

Maxey sank onto the corner of his bed, wanted to stretch out full length on it. "So what is it you want from me?"

"Could you please back up my story to the police? That you and I were suspicious of Stamp because I overheard him on the switchboard? And that I brought the stun gun to your room because I heard you scream?"

"Oh, Grady, this isn't fair. I feel so awful, I just want it all to be over. But to help you lie, and then to let you go on using this—this—snoop equipment on unsuspecting customers—"

"I won't! You don't need to worry about that at all, because Winnie—that's my mom—is selling the motel—next week, probably—and I'll be standing in the unemployment line." He smiled an appealing, earnest smile. When it didn't immediately win her over, he added, "If you don't believe me, you can ask Winnie."

"Okay, okay," she capitulated. "Just call the damn police, will you?"

They waited companionably for the police to arrive. Grady tipped back with his feet on the desk and Maxey lay with a cold washcloth draped over her eyes.

"So I should get five hundred bucks for Jim Donovan and two hundred bucks for Jerald Stamp," Grady counted his chickens.

"I don't think there's any money in the Stamp bank account to pay a reward, and besides, the person offering it, Rita, is dead."

"I won't depend on that, then. But still, the five hundred that you folks at the newspaper were offering will come in handy."

Maxey sighed with real regret. "Sorry, Grady. I'd like you to get a reward. But you haven't helped us solve Jim's murder. Stamp didn't kill Jim Donovan."

"He didn't? What makes you think that?"

"Stamp told me."

"And you *believed* him?"

Finally she could hear sirens, far, far away. She lifted a corner of the washcloth and squinted at her watch. Ten-oh-seven. She'd give anything to be sitting at home with a frosty root beer, watching Channel Four news.

Tomorrow night, she'd be on the news.

"You can't really believe anything that guy says," Grady persisted.

"Why would he fib about it? He'd already admitted to me that he murdered his wife. So what's one more murder? I wasn't going to be in any condition to tell anyone anyway." An involuntary shudder racked her sore back.

"Well, if he didn't do it, who did?"

It was a hypothetical question. They lapsed into silence, listening to the growing howl of patrol cars, ambulances, and Jerald Stamp's dog.

Of course Grady wouldn't let her receive the police here in his clandestine boudoir. He urged her up and out into the office and perched her on his creaky, unpadded desk chair. Red, white, and blue lights strafed the windows, and the sound of slamming doors and thudding feet made Maxey want to stand up and cheer.

But not badly enough. She propped her chin on her hand, elbow on the desk.

For the next half hour the office swarmed with strangers in various uniforms. Rushing in, rushing out, asking her questions, asking Grady questions. Polite. Grim. Efficient, in spite of appearances, she bet. One of them brought her a leaking Styrofoam cup of steaming black coffee, which Maxey welcomed with profuse thanks and the promise of her firstborn child.

When they retrieved Stamp from fourteen, Grady stood by the window, giving Maxey a running commentary. "He's walking on his own, but there's a cop on either side helping him. He's kind of gray, but maybe it's the lights. And that stuff on his face is peeling off like he's a zombie or something."

Tipping her head to get the last sip of coffee, Maxey felt a tweak of pain between her shoulder blades and wished Stamp the very worst of everything.

"Now he's in the ambulance and the cops got in, too. There they go. Lights but no siren. Hey, there's somebody out there taking pictures. You think it's a reporter?"

Maxey started to shrug and thought better of it. At least her nose didn't hurt. It was numb.

Grady jumped out of the way as two uniformed policemen and one uniformed emergency medic tramped into the office. They all looked purposefully at Maxey.

"You want an ambulance over to Poudre Valley?" one officer asked. "Or can you ride in the back of a cruiser?"

"Hey, give me directions and I can drive over in my own car. Better yet, I'll go home to my own hospital."

Ignoring her bravado, the one who'd asked told the other one to put her in the back of his cruiser. Helping her up, he added, "Is there someone we could notify for you, Ms. Burnell?"

Her first thought was Sam Russell. He'd have to be informed of the Stamp/Donovan development anyway. But she hated to intrude on his headache. Reece? It would be nice to have him come rushing to her side with words of encouragement and arms both gentle and strong. That was one of his biggest talents—comforting women. On second thought, she didn't want Reece.

Well then, how about—

The men shuffled their feet, impatient to get on with the wrap-up. But Maxey was frozen in the awful realization that there wasn't anyone she could call. Her closest relative—both geographically and by blood—was an aunt in Omaha; her closest female friend had just gotten married and become a mother without informing Maxey. For the first time since the ordeal began, she felt an overwhelming need to weep.

Which made her all the more determined not to give in to weakness.

Stretching her sore lips into a smile, she wise-cracked, "Moe's too lazy to answer the phone." And then: "My cat," she explained to all the blank faces.

❖　❖　❖

X rays showed that her spine and neck were okay. A doctor gave her nose a local anesthetic and then used sophisticated tools—his two hands—to pop the bone back into place. He assured her that once the puffiness and discoloration went away, she'd be beautiful.

"That's super—I've always wanted to be beautiful," she said in a variation of the old now-I-can-play-piano joke.

She slept off the emotional and physical damage in one of the hospital's crisp, white beds; and in the morning she checked herself out, found a phone booth in the lobby, and began the first day of the rest of her life.

18

 Maxey phoned Reece to tell him she'd be late coming to work and why.

Then she phoned Sam to tell him the trip to Grand Junction was no longer necessary and why.

Next she phoned for a taxi to take her to the Come On Inn to pick up her car.

Mentally checking off her things-to-do list, she stepped through the hospital's discreet automatic doors into a perfect Colorado day, all blue sky and caressing sunshine. Down at the end of that list she reminded herself to find a friend.

Sam had asked her to stop by his office when she got back to town. She didn't even go home first to freshen up. If he was repelled by her down-and-dirty appearance, the hell with him—him and his ugly wardrobe.

The female receptionist gave Maxey a curious once-over, and the two detectives at their desks in the communal office nodded and looked away fast, but Sam didn't bat an eye. He glanced up from paperwork and motioned to a chair.

Making a final notation with his pen, he shut the folder and gave her his attention. "You look like you had a tiger by the tail."

"Yeah. To make matters worse, he was an empty tiger."

Sam thought about that. The two detectives scraped their chairs back, discussing lunch.

"So, you okay?" Sam asked.

"I will be, about tomorrow."

"And Stamp didn't kill Donovan, huh?"

"I don't think so."

"We'll check for an alibi."

"He was probably with Anita Oakley."

"We'll check."

"How's your headache?"

"Gone."

The two detectives went out the door, calling to someone down the hall, laughing at whatever was said back.

Sam put the pen on top of the folder, taking pains to line it up in the exact center. Then he pushed away his chair and stood. With a face blank as a Greek statue's, he circled around to Maxey, urged her up with a hand under her elbow, and carefully took her into his arms. For the next few minutes he simply held her.

Maxey felt like a desert survivor who had just found an oasis.

The week ticked by. Maxey granted interviews to local media, sharing enough information about Saturday night's adventure to get publicity for her own paper, saving the best details for a first-person account in the *Regard*. Respecting the agreement she'd made with Grady, she reported that he'd heard her scream, not elaborating on exactly *how* he'd heard it.

Reece was so solicitous of her the first few days at the office that she had to resort to an outrageously unfair insult—"Your writing sucks like a chest wound"—to make him stop.

She began to feel good again. The brush with mortality had heightened all her senses. And all her appetites. Accordingly, once she had put the paper to bed on Wednesday, Maxey went home to phone Sam and see if she could do the same with him.

"Come over," she invited huskily into the receiver. "I'll make you—dinner."

"Something wrong with your throat?" he asked without a trace of solicitude.

"No," she snapped. "Are you coming or not?"

"I'm not sure I can make it tonight, Max. I got a lot of paperwork to catch up—"

"I plan to give a whole new meaning to the term 'private investigation.'"

There was silence on the line while he processed this new information. "Uh, Maxey?"

"Mmm?"

"What time should I be there?"

"Yesterday wouldn't be too soon," she intoned, and then spoiled the whole seductive bit by giggling.

Afterward—after he'd arrived within the hour and agreed he wasn't hungry either—they lay on the damp, tangled sheets and watched the ceiling slowly fade to black.

"You going to go let the cat in?" Sam asked.

"What?" she said, half-asleep.

"He's been yowling for the last ten minutes."

"Uh. I thought that was you."

"Very funny."

Even as she was grinning she wanted to cry. For the brevity of life and the interminable pursuit of happiness.

Thursday afternoon Sam phoned her at the office. "Thought you'd be interested in this, Max."

She had stopped trying to correct his name for her. In fact, she'd decided she didn't hate it nearly as much as she used to.

"We located a guy who admits to phoning Donovan once with a threatening message. Says he talked to a woman—must be you. Want to come see if you recognize the voice?"

It was hopeless. She'd said she'd know it again, but it had been too long ago. They had the suspect say similar words on an extension phone while she listened. All she could conclude was that it *could* have been the same voice.

He had an alibi for the morning of Jim's death—in jail on a DUI. Sam let him go with a warning to stay available.

"His name's Dee Wilburt. Mean anything to you?" Sam said when they were alone in his office, exchanging smoldering looks across his desk.

"No. How'd you find him?"

"He found us. Said his conscience made him get in touch, but more likely it was the possible five-hundred-dollar reward that was nagging at him. His story is that a stranger made him do it."

"Uh-huh."

"For twenty bucks. Supposed to be a practical joke on a friend, Donovan. Call him up and say something terse and nasty. End of job."

"What did this employer look like?"

"Average height, average weight, average age. A beard."

"A beard! Well, hey, what more do you need?"

"This is a college town, for chrissake. Do you know how many men have beards in a college town?"

"Detective work is such a drag."

"I'm in it for the fringe benefits," he said, winking to be sure she got his drift.

☼   ☼   ☼

Two things happened Friday.

First, Lucky, the mailperson, came in and dropped a bundle of mail under Maxey's nose. Ordinarily Maxey would have set it aside until she'd finished the article she was writing. But this time an unusual envelope on top, a textured blue number ten with a St. Louis postmark, addressed to Jim, attracted her curiosity.

The letterhead was the Nieberding Clinic. The letter was form, from a dot-matrix printer. *Dear Mr. Donovan: Thank you for your donation. If we can be of any further service to you, do not hesitate to call on us. Sincerely yours, Lawrence Alvin Nieberding.*

"Reece," she said, raising her voice. He was across the room sorting through the clip-art library. "Did you ever hear of a Nieberding Clinic? In St. Louis?"

He considered. "Don't think so."

"Did you ever show the police that plane ticket to St. Louis that was in Jim's jacket pocket?"

"Huh?"

"You were going to see if they could find out why he went there."

"Forgot." He stopped shuffling pages and lifted one to study in the light, ignoring Maxey in general.

She tucked the letter into the side pocket of her shoulder bag. Something to research at the public library.

The second significant occurrence took place

when Reece was out to lunch and Maxey was standing in the office doorway, sipping at a cup of coffee and people watching. The usual unusual mix of housewives, college kids, hippies, and punkers were out in full force. One of the colorful figures passing by sent her a furtive look, as if afraid of being hailed.

"Kim!" Maxey did hail. "Ms. Oviatt. Please, could I talk to you for a minute?"

The young woman stopped and turned around warily. Wearing an ankle-length purple sundress and hoop earrings as big as bracelets, she looked less like a flower child this time, more like a Gypsy.

"I'm sorry if I said something to offend you last time," Maxey placated. "Won't you come in and have a cup of coffee? There's something else I'd like to ask you."

Kim frowned up the street as if about to decline. "I've got a minute," she said, stepping under the shade of the roof.

Drawing her the promised coffee, Maxey said, "As you know, I had trouble with the reading you did on the poison-pen notes." She glided back, watching the overfull cup. "What I'm wondering is"—she gave Kim custody of the coffee and smiled encouragement—"could those have been written in a disguised hand? Someone deliberately writing a different way from normal, to keep the reader from recognizing the writing?"

"Oh, sure." Kim sipped and made a face.

"So if the writing was disguised, that would explain why you were misled about the writer's character. You said he was cool and calm and pleasant in general. But the writer might really be just the opposite, if he wasn't writing in his usual way."

Kim had begun shaking her head three sentences ago. "That isn't how it works. To the untrained eye, the writing might appear different than the person's normal handwriting, but to the graphoanalyst, there's no difference. The reading will be the same for the same person. Until, of course, he has a change of personality, in which case the handwriting will also, automatically, change."

Maxey could feel herself about to say something that would further alienate Ms. Oviatt. "Here," she said instead, sweeping up a page of handwritten notes that Reece had left on her desk, suggestions for articles for next week's *Regard*. "What can you tell me about the person who wrote this?"

She'd just see if Kim could correctly describe Reece.

"Intelligent. Quiet. Compassionate. Concerned about money. Self-controlled."

"Ha!" Maxey couldn't stop herself from exclaiming. "This man is a womanizer and a gambler. He has no more self-control than a gnat."

"Maybe he isn't self-controlled in some areas of his life," Kim said, defending her interpretation, "but he is in others. He probably works hard. And he pays off his debts. Because he's stubborn. See here how his crossbars on his *t*'s bow down? Every one of them."

Maxey thought probably Kim's *t* crossbars bowed down, too.

"And he's an optimist," Kim went on. "The way his writing goes uphill."

"Fascinating," Maxey lied, suddenly sorry she'd wasted everyone's time like this. "Well, thank you so much for your help."

Taking her cue, Kim set down the half-finished coffee and started for the door. "Was this a test?" she demanded.

"Maybe, in a way."

"You wanted to see if I'd know it was the same writer." Kim nodded, emphasizing the accusation.

"No, I—"

"Well, you can't expect me to come right out and say it: 'These samples are from the same guy.'"

"No, I wouldn't expect—"

"All I can say is they're real similar personalities. Except this one writes uphill like he's happy, and that other one wrote downhill like he was unhappy."

Kim flounced out the door without benefit of good-bye. Maxey sank onto her chair and stared into space.

Snatching up a memo pad and pen, she scribbled what she recalled of Kim's analysis. Intelligent. Stubborn. Optimistic. Quiet. Self-controlled. Compassionate. Concerned about money.

Feeling like a perverted Girl Scout, she ticked

these off: a successful murderer is intelligent, stubborn, optimistic, quiet. Compassionate? Sure, in the case of mercy killings. Maxey couldn't correlate any compassion with exploding one good man into nothingness. Concerned about money? Oh, yeah. She had never asked Reece about the alleged gambling debts. She'd figured he'd laugh and deny it and she still wouldn't know.

But Reece and Jim had been friends, damn it! And Maxey could no more picture Reece blowing up Jim than she could imagine Jim rigging Reece's Fiat to explode.

Reece took a two-hour lunch, which was just as well, because when he did return, Maxey had a hard time keeping her eyes away from him.

Once her speculations boiled over in a blurted question. "Didn't you have a beard this spring?"

Bemused by the editing he was doing at that moment, he didn't seem to notice the oddity of the remark. "Mmm, I don't remember."

"Yes, you do. You did. About three months ago you shaved it off."

"They itch in hot weather." Then his eyes sharpened on her, and she swiveled her chair away to do some filing.

Maxey locked the office door and strode off. The mall was tuning up for evening; fragmented stanzas of folk and country and jazz, guitar and banjo and trumpet, floated through the canyon of buildings. A clown tipped his fluorescent-pink toupee to Maxey as she dodged pedestrian traffic. Leaving the ambience of Pearl Street and crossing Walnut was like leaving a theater's suspension of disbelief and returning to reality.

She jaywalked Canyon Boulevard and angled through the public-library parking lot. A man approaching in the dying light, books stacked under one arm, the other hand in a pants pocket, accelerated Maxey's heart. Jim.

But of course it wasn't, and she remembered Sam's rueful comment about how many college-town residents are bearded men.

Yet another hirsute male was sitting at the reference librarian's desk. He helped her find a directory of medical facilities of the United States.

Nieberding Clinic. Her fingernail traced the name, address, phone number, director's name, and dropped a line to reveal the speciality of the house: *for the research and treatment of amyotrophic lateral sclerosis, commonly known as "Lou Gehrig's disease."*

Her backbone slapped the back of her chair and she stared, sightless, across the quiet room.

Compassion, she thought. Oh, God, Reece.

Maxey walked the eleven blocks home. At the foot of the stairs that she had never minded before, she paused, gazing up, remembering how Jim had backed away from them. I would have brought lunch down to the porch! she scolded his ghost.

Moe wasn't the kind of cat one could easily scoop up and nuzzle, but Maxey managed to do it, and his ponderous furry body overhanging her arms made her smile. Setting him down to a bowl of giblets 'n' more, she trudged to the bedroom.

Jim's notebook of poems was on top of the bureau where she'd left it the evening she brought it home from the cabin. It fell open to the same page she had begun and never finished reading:

> *Three miles away my friend*
> *Occupies a bed more versatile than she.*
> *Different snow slides past her pane,*
> *Melting on her eyes.*
> *Petrified*
> *Of fire*
> *Of catching cold*
> *Of everything*
> *She waits.*
> *I will break into the stagnant room*
> *With words and coffee on my breath,*
> *Rattling chains of jewelry and keys,*
> *Never looking at my watch*
> *To calculate what's left.*

Jim's neat handwriting sloped downhill.

She couldn't wait till morning; she had to settle this now. Grabbing up billfold and car keys,

Maxey was halfway out the door when a memory of how she'd felt in that motel room with Jerald Stamp stopped her—long enough to phone Sam's home answering machine to leave Reece's number on it.

19

She'd never been to Reece's current place, wasn't sure he still lived at the address noted in her little red book, since he'd been staging a running battle with his landlady. The street was one of the old, narrow ones on the west side, with cottonwood trees, upheaving sidewalks, and a view of neighbors' roofs. The house was a two-story painted lady in need of paint, and maybe not much of a lady either. Reece's number was nailed to the clapboard wall beside an outside stairway with a wood banister that shook under her hand.

She began to climb, noticing that this side of the building had been recently painted a whiter shade of white. Perhaps it foretold a general fix-up for the old girl.

Feeling as if she were going to the dentist,

Maxey knocked on the glass-windowed door at the top. After a silence she did it again, harder.

"In a minute!" Reece called.

She held to the rail and gazed down at her little car, pretty sure she'd looked for her last bomb under it.

The door beside her rattled open. "Maxey! Wow. Welcome. Come in, come in." He was wearing a brown plaid flannel robe and backless leather slippers. He rushed to say, "You caught me on the way to a shower. Have a seat."

On the verge of apologizing for barging in, she yanked herself short. Whose fault was it anyway?

The room was neater than she'd expected. Its only real clutter was cozy things—books, newspapers, cushions, records, and tapes. The highbacked wing chair she chose to sit in was comfortable. Reece dropped onto his flowered couch, arms outstretched along the back, the picture of ease, except for his watchful eyes.

Crossing her knees, she reluctantly brought the meeting to order. "I'm not afraid of you, Reece. But Sam does know where I am, just in case."

He snorted his disbelief. "I admit you're a tempting dish, especially now that you've got that cute little zigzag in the middle of your nose. But I sure wouldn't ever seduce a lady who didn't want—"

"We aren't talking about that."

"What *are* we talking about?" He wore that choirboy expression that she had loved until she found out how many other women had also loved it.

"We're talking about Jim's murder."

"Oh. Okay."

"What I haven't figured out for sure is motive. Was it Tessa?"

His blank stare was very convincing. "Was it Tessa what?"

"Did you want her for more than a one-night stand? Because of her million-dollar deals? And Jim wouldn't divorce her?"

"Maxey," he said as gently as if she were a madwoman to be humored. "I never laid eyes—or anything else—on Tessa Donovan till the day you and I stumbled on her at the cabin."

"One motive down." Maxey counted on her fingers. "Two to go. You stole or borrowed money from Jim. To pay off your debts. Maybe you owed the wrong guys in Las Vegas, had to have the money right away and Jim wouldn't stand for—"

"Maxey!" Humoring had given way to outrage. "What is this? In the first place Jim didn't have any money, and in the next place I didn't need any that bad. Not bad enough to blow up the poor guy. Maxey, for gosh sake listen to yourself. This is crazy."

She rubbed at pain in the nape of her neck and said wearily, "Good. I'm glad you didn't kill him for reasons one or two. Now we come to three."

"Maxey, what's got into you?"

"Did Jim ask you to kill him or did you just decide to do it on your own?"

Reece's face blushed red and washed sickly

white. But when he held up a supplicating hand, it was steady. "You're going to have to say what you're thinking straight out, because I don't have any idea in the world what led to you accusing me like this."

She leaned forward, watching his eyes. "Are you saying you didn't know Jim had amyotrophic lateral sclerosis?"

He blinked. "Good God, what's that?"

"Lou Gehrig's disease."

Slumping back on the couch, he gave every impression of being stunned. As silence stretched, Maxey noticed the wind picking up outside, a clock ticking, snatches of music wafting from another room.

"You think I performed a mercy killing," Reece said. "To save Jim from slow, terminal paralysis."

"Your handwriting shows you're compassionate." She said it quietly and with a thin smile, turning flippancy into a compliment. "Come on, Reece. You can let down your hair with me. I understand. I don't think I could have done it, and I don't like the method, but it was a brave thing to do."

He stood up, motioning for her to stay where she was. "I want to show you something."

Maxey bounced to the edge of her chair, prepared to roll either direction if he came back shooting.

The something was a someone, a tiny doll of a girl in an oversized terrycloth robe, who followed Reece into the living room clinging to his hand.

When her dark eyes met Maxey's, Maxey decided the "girl" must be at least twenty-five.

"Maxey, this is Marie. Marie, Maxey." He wrapped his arm protectively around Marie's shoulders and hugged her one quick hug. "I met her in Vegas. She's a dancer."

"Oh, I can see that. I bet she can limbo like anything."

Marie's shy smile never wavered. Maybe she couldn't speak English.

"Do you want to talk about Jim or not?" Reece asked. "I'm trying to explain things to you. That one trip to Las Vegas is the only time I've ever been there. Leo Crown's got it all ass backward about my gambling. I played the slots, mostly, and came out even. Marie has a younger brother, though, who needed bailing out of an injudicious binge of blackjack, and I cosigned a loan with her, is probably what Crown got wind of."

Marie's long brown hair was exactly the wanton mane that Maxey had wanted when she was a teen, which was probably why she felt this strong urge to pull it out.

Reece said, "Marie is my alibi. We were together all night and next morning right up to the time Jim died."

"For what that's worth," Maxey scoffed. "Lovers alibi-ing each other are always taken with a grain of salt."

"Yes, but in this case there's a third witness."

"Oooh, kinky."

"A previous, uh, friend of mine surprised us. I'd forgotten Lisa had a key."

Marie elevated her shoulders and snickered into her hands like a four-year-old.

"After I ushered Lisa out, she sat at the foot of my stairs, telling the world she'd stay there until I should come to my senses and kick Marie out. When we did finally emerge after daylight, she was busy spray-painting an obscenity on the side of the house."

Maxey shook her head, gave up, and giggled with Marie. "Why didn't you tell Sam Russell?"

"I would have, if he ever charged me and I needed to save myself. Actually I was scared Lisa would see it as a chance for revenge. I was afraid she'd swear she saw me sneak out and that I was gone plenty long enough to commit a murder."

Sighing, Maxey stood up, gave Reece a sad smile. "Well, I'll see you tomorrow. Nice meeting you, Marie."

"Oh, sure." Marie spoke up at last. "You can come by anytime." She had a Brooklyn accent as broad as a bridge.

Maxey had one foot inside the Toyota when Reece whistled at her from his little porch. "Sam Russell's on the phone."

"Ask him to meet me at my house," she shouted. "Tell him you're harmless."

Maxey parked in front of her house, and the shadow on the front steps stood up to meet her.

"I guess since you got here within thirty minutes, I have to pay for it," she said to Sam, touching the reassuring substance of his arm.

"Satisfaction guaranteed," he said, swinging the arm around her shoulders and strolling her across the porch. "What's up?"

She jabbed the key in the lock. "I solved your case for you—Jim's death."

"Come on—on top of your Rita Stamp triumph? You're in the wrong business, lady."

They climbed the stairs, Sam's palm across her bottom, giving lift. "You must live close to have beat me home," she said, feeling each muscle in her body working to drag her up.

It seemed very important, now, to know his address, his birthday, his goal in life, just as she wanted to tell him all about herself.

Because she didn't mind living alone, but she didn't want to die alone.

Maxey wriggled out of range onto the cold side of the bed, not ready to enjoy life yet. "Will the insurance company refuse to honor Jim's policy? If they do, the *Regard* will have to fold."

"A reputable company would pay off. For good public relations if for no other reason. Who knows what Crown's outfit will do?" He reeled her toward him again, tipped her onto her back, bent over to brush a kiss on her abused nose.

"It's not so much that I want to own the newspaper, it's just the thought of Jim trying so hard to cover up the actual circumstances of his death. Do you realize"—her voice wobbled up the scale—"he's such a nice guy he even waited for a rainy night, to make sure the explosion wouldn't start a forest fire?"

"Yeah," Sam growled, wiping her bangs out of her eyes, exposing her forehead the way she'd always hated. She had more important things to hate right now.

"And Moe. He wanted to be sure Moe got taken care of. That's why he wrote a fake vet appointment on his calendar. To tell me he had a cat."

Sam's thumb smoothed her eyebrow. "Shh, I know, it's okay," he consoled her.

"Writing himself threatening letters, for godsake. Hiring that guy Dee Wilburt to make a sinister phone call." Maxey sniffed. "I want to collect on the insurance because I want Jim to have succeeded."

She drew feathery hearts on Sam's bare chest. In a few months Jim would not have been able to move his fingers in so simple an exercise as this. How horrible that while he still could use his hands, he'd used them to spill gasoline and wire a spark plug and twist a key in an ignition.

Sam let her cry and then he let her sleep.

Grady had spent most of the week dismantling and packing electronic components. It had been like burying friends who'd fallen victim to some disaster.

Now he sat beside his mother on one side of the kitchen table, and Mr. Randolph Newby sat on the other. Having signed her name to a dozen different legal papers, Winnie was treating herself to a cigarette. Mr. Newby reached into his black vinyl carry case and reverently withdrew a long, white check.

"This is all yours, Mrs. Feders," he said, passing it over.

Winnie clicked her tongue and swung her head, as if the figure was a big surprise and not precisely the purchase price both parties had agreed upon days ago.

"Look at that, Grady. There's your inheritance. If I don't spend it all first." And she rumbled one of her rare laughs.

Mr. Newby tidied up the papers into his case and gave the table a rap with his fist, a gesture of satisfaction and finality. "So, Mr. Feders. Do you have any future plans?"

None that's your business, he wanted to say. But there was Winnie's right hand resting next to his left, holding a lighted cigarette. She never had, but that didn't mean she never would.

Prudently he answered, "I've been looking in the want ads for a motel manager job, but so far—"

"We'll probably put an addition on fairly soon," Newby cut in. "On the back. Maybe a second story. This location is bound to appeal to real-estate agents and other upscale folks. We don't want an office building, we want an office complex." He showed all his teeth in a smile so brief—blink and you'd have missed it.

Winnie crushed out her cigarette—in an ashtray—and stowed the cashier's check in her purse.

"So, Mr. Feders," Newby droned on. "What would you think of a job with us?"

Grady wanted to punch something or someone. He laced his fingers and said, "I'm not much of a carpenter. I could maybe help string electricity."

Newby's laugh was as abbreviated as his smile. "No. I mean we need a resident building manager. Someone we can depend on to keep close tabs on the entire place. All the offices. Day and night."

Grady blinked. Then he grinned from ear to ear.

"Mr. Newby, I'm your man," he said.